Blood on the Bridal Wreath

M E FULLER

ISBN: 978-1-7370757-0-7

DEDICATION

For Diane Schlagel, my 2020 life jacket.

ACKNOWLEDGMENTS

Thank you Melissa Birch, Donna Bohn, Daniel Francis, Charlie Johnson, Jan Kurtz, Lauren Nickish, Darrell Pederson, and Donna Salli for feedback and proofreading and general support with generous enthusiasm.

CHAPTER I
Blood on the Bridal Wreath

A basket of freshly harvested, young and tender turnip greens at her feet, Mrs. Julian Stanche stood to stretch. "Oh, my achin', achin'," she mumbled to no one, except maybe The Cat. The Cat was a nine-year-old striped tabby, always underfoot. Mrs. Julian Stanche—or Justy as she was called by the more informal types about town—stepped on The Cat's tail at the height of her stretch. Both parties screamed. The Cat, with claws extended, etched deep grooves into the flesh of Mrs. Stanche's shapely left leg, drawing blood. "Oh, Lordy," she exclaimed, thinking instead what she would never utter aloud, *Damnable cat!* The Cat launched itself off her leg to race toward a nearby bridal wreath bush in full bloom.

Just then, the handsome new Episcopal reverend, Father Persons and his beautiful, buxom wife of twenty-five years, Lucille—or Busty as she was called by the more informal types about town—passed by the front yard picket fence.

"Did you hear that?" Lucille's voice was high and thin and urgent. She pushed through the white, four-slat gate without waiting for her husband to reply.

"Hello? Are you all right?" Lucille cried out as she rounded the backside of the house, approaching Mrs. Stanche's garden.

The Cat flew past her, yowling as if a territorial battle with the neighbor's yellow cat were in full sway. "Oh!" Lucille jumped with fright, tripped over The Cat, and fell, face first, into the bridal wreath bush, sending The Cat scurrying and screaming, under the back-porch steps.

"My dear!" Father Persons, reaching his wife just as she plummeted into the bridal wreath blossoms, managed to catch her before she reached the ground. Pulling her back toward himself, wishing to soothe her and examine her wounds, he heard Mrs. Julian Stanche scream again. Mrs. Stanche, her face stricken and ashy white, her left leg covered in blood both oozing and dried, extended her arm toward her beloved bridal wreath. "Oh, Lord above," she shrieked, "Is that *your* blood?"

Father Persons, his wife firmly grasped in his arms, took in the sight that was Mrs. Stanche's bloody leg and the bridal wreath bush, one side of which was well crushed and covered in what looked to be blood, bright red against the stark white blossoms. This was certainly not the blood of his wife who sustained a few minor scratches in her fall.

Father Persons set his wife on her feet, brushed her off, and with loving tenderness, inspected each small abrasion on her face. "It is not my wife's blood, Mrs. Stanche." And in the most accusatory of tones, he continued, "What happened here?"

Mrs. Stanche stammered, "I… I… I don't know. I was in my garden, harvesting turnip greens when I stepped on The Cat's tail, and then this happened. She swept her hand across her bloodied leg. And now you're here and I see this!" She stares without a gesture at her bush.

"Well, Mrs. Stanche, this blood is fresh, and appears to be

fresher than the blood on your leg!" The Father's tone was unkind. "I'm going to call the police."

As he reached for his phone, his lovely wife stopped him. "Please don't, dear." All could see the relief on Mrs. Stanche's face. "Officers will trample Mrs. Stanche's yard and garden. They'll make a terrible mess. Besides, the blood could have come from anywhere."

The reverend paused to study his wife. "That much blood? Someone was killed here or mortally wounded at the very least. I'm calling the police!"

At that precise moment, Larry Grainger, the local organic farmer who'd lost his dear wife only two years before, came strolling around the corner of Mrs. Stanche's house. Mrs. Stanche, ashen and bloodied, Mrs. Persons, scratched and shaky, and Father Persons, his determined hand on his cell phone, looked up at once to see Larry looking at them.

"What in the hell has happened here?" Larry Grainger was the best-looking man in four adjoining counties, and he had a thing for Mrs. Julian Stanche, a widow of nine years.

Mrs. Stanche never used her given name of Gloria because, as she said many times to gossiping ladies of the church, *"I don't need a man. I don't want a man. I don't want to give any indication at any time, place, or instance, that a man could entertain the idea of me as escort or companion,"* so she was averse and perhaps even ignorant of Grainger's intentions. Yet Grainger busied himself, in his free time—all of it—at the work of wearing down Gloria's defenses. Today, he arrived at her home with a gift of rare, heirloom, scarlet runner bean seeds, the blooms well known to attract hummingbirds, butterflies, and bees.

Mrs. Julian Stanche needed no additional opportunities to draw pollinators to her garden. Her garden in bloom was alive with all manner of industrious insects, hoarding and swapping pollen. But Larry, a stranger to subtlety, eager to woo her, would not overlook a chance to insist himself upon her good nature, as a woman and fellow gardener.

As an organic farmer, Larry was savvy in the ways of safe yet effective fertilizing of crops for the greatest yield. He could handle a rebuff or setback from a spotted wing drosophila or aphid. A man of patience and persistence, he knew how to coexist with or conquer threats to his farm, but in a good way, as he was so fond of saying.

Like a bee needing a coax to find his Hubbard and acorn squash at first blossom, so too would the staunchly adverse Mrs. Stanch require a soft touch of encouragement. His intent to transplant the beautiful backyard gardener to his own eighty acres of farmland would succeed. He believed this with all his heart, for one so handsome had never lost a game of love or lust.

All eyes were on Larry now. All lips were still. Behind him, a wooden ladder came down, crashing on top of the back-porch steps. A sound of splintering was followed by a curse.

"Dammit!"

This was followed by another scream from The Cat, now on a dead run from beneath the steps to some other, more distant, hiding place. Larry turned toward the crashing sound to see Hank Broden, the village's most popular handyman, known for his craftsmanship and fair prices, sprawled on blood-soaked ground.

"Dammit!" Hank mumbled again into the moist dirt. Larry raced to help him up from his fall.

At that moment everyone noticed, just beyond the blood-covered Broden, an oft-used metal paint bucket emptied of its contents when it too, fell from the ladder. First a unified gasp, then a unified "Ahhhh," rose from the bystanders in Mrs. Stanche's backyard. The blood on the bridal wreath was not in fact, blood at all. Reverend Persons dropped his phone, set to dial 911. A faint background voice could be heard, had anyone been listening.

"Hello? Is everything all right?" This was quickly followed by the sound of sirens wailing from a squad car dispatched for an unknown emergency. The sounds of brakes screeching, car doors slamming, and noisy boots running, were followed by a most insistent pounding away on Mrs. Stanche's front door.

"Open up! Police!"

Unhappily for The Cat, its haven was through the front entrance cat door. It had nearly settled itself when the police shouted, just outside. The Cat, all hairs flared, not bothering with a hiss or snarl, disappeared to the upper regions of the house.

Cries of "back here!" could not be heard above the din. The Reverend's wife took flight around the house to signal the two uniformed officers to please, quiet down.

"Sssssh!" She mouthed, waving her arms at them, attempting to catch their attention.

Officers Franklin and Lorde had given up their pounding and readied themselves to break down the door when they spied Mrs. Persons and her frantic waving. Her mouth was so contorted by the shushing they believed she may be suffering a stroke. In a moment they were both upon her, one at her head, one at her feet, wrestling her to the ground as she would not cease her flailing.

"Stop that!" The Reverend shouted at the officers. "Unleash my wife!"

He had followed her and watched in horror as the officers took his beloved to the ground. Both officers looked up at the shouting to see Reverend Persons and the others, including Hank Borden, coated in red paint. They promptly released Lucille Persons.

"What is going on here?"

Detective Franklin demanded an explanation for the emergency call while Detective Lorde helped Lucille to her feet, never once lifting his eyes from her most alluring cleavage peeking out just enough from the edge of her knit top—just enough to tantalize, but certainly not meant to tempt.

"Do you need an ambulance?" Detective Franklin noticed the fallen ladder, the spilled bucket of paint, and Hank's paint-covered overalls.

"No sir," Hank replied with the utmost deference to Detective Franklin's authority. "No sir," he repeated. "I jes fall off o' my ladder. Jes need to shake meself off is all."

Detective Franklin nodded, folded up her notebook, and adjusted the hardware about her hips. "All right then. If there's nothing else."

The lot of them shook their heads and waved the officers on their way.

"Oh my," exclaimed Mrs. Stanche as she turned back to her garden. "My greens are all wilted. I must get them into the pot to steam." With that, she turned away from the others, wishing them to leave her alone to deal with the mess in her yard.

"I'll take care o' the mess, ma'am." Hank cried out after her.

"Let me help you with that." Larry was at Mrs. Stanche's elbow, his hands on her garden basket before she could object. She pulled her elbow away from his grasp, though he clung to her basket's bottom.

"Thank you, Mr. Grainger, but I don't need your help." Her tone, she felt, was sufficiently dismissive. She pulled her basket from his grasp, then turned her back on the two men remaining in the yard. Gloria walked up the back-porch steps and entered her house to calm down, stew her greens, and rest from the unexpected and most unwelcomed chaos of the morning.

CHAPTER 2
The Buffalo View Village Picnic

The small prairie village of Buffalo View was established by Swedes to the detriment of its first indigenous peoples. The Swedish settlers in times past, though conflicted about the Indian wars in these parts, wanted land more than they wanted to satisfy their Christian duty to love one another. As luck would have it, the Indigenous folks in Buffalo View survived the various and numerous clashes and the invaders were easy about forgetting the whole thing, thereby accomplishing the Lord's commandment to love. This greater love was exemplified in the familial lines of descent falling from the union of Elmore Blue Fox and Sylvie Johannson.

The mix of Lakota and Swede made for the most interesting church basement buffet suppers of milky bison meatballs, unseasoned buffalo and prairie turnip hand pies (made with Betty Jorgeson's lefse recipe from 1822) slathered in gravy, wojapi, and fruit soups. Everybody's favorite, of course, was the creamy corn pudding. Elmore's great-great niece, Tiffaney, was famous for her stuffed pumpkin dish, filled with wild rice blended into cream of mushroom soup.

The deep and abiding love held within the Blue Fox family was a model for all to follow, though most did not, at least not at home. However, in public, familial displays of admiration and togetherness rose to a level of sheer outlandishness, as every family strove to be the one family by which love could be the measure. With summer approaching, and with it, the Buffalo View Village picnic, families convened to devise how they may represent and flaunt their superior love and devotion of one another, thereby being the most talked about and respected family of the year.

This concerned Mrs. Julian Stanche only in the effect that the Buffalo View Village picnic was more than an opportunity for family posturing. The townsfolk were competitive, not only family against family, but in any and all ways they could vie to be voted the best—even against their own kin. There would be cake decorating and stick throwing and baby weighing and pig racing. Whatever rivalry could be accomplished, there would be an event with a trophy for the winner.

Gloria had no family hereabouts. What she lacked in familial displays of adoration, she made up for in spectacular prize-winning garden blooms and vegetables. This year she planned to exhibit her red cactus zinnias and early beets for pickling. She had intended a breathtaking dried floral wreath arrangement featuring sprays of Spirea japonica, (bridal wreath to the commoner), interwoven with red and yellow tea roses. With the bridal wreath bush spattered red by Hank Broden's clumsiness, well, she had a bad taste in her mouth about it and changed course without missing a step. Mrs. Stanche was nothing if not flexible in her thinking.

Gloria stood up from her repose and rumination. The bridal wreath bush needed attention. She could not have her yard so besmirched, and she did not trust Hank Borden to clean up his mess to her satisfaction.

Something other than her bush. nagged at her innermost thoughts. The harder she thought, the more she felt that something was wrong. She began to pace, her face frowning, her eyes focused straight ahead, then down at her feet.

"Oh, no," she exclaimed at the site of her feet in a voice loud enough to startle herself. She was still wearing her garden shoes while pacing back and forth on her pristine floral carpet, specially chosen for its hues of soft blue, green, and gold. She followed her footprints, back and forth, then out toward the kitchen. The filth was everywhere. Gloria sighed and plopped herself back down into a favorite easy chair for further ruminating.

"What's wrong with me?" She spoke the words out loud and frightened herself with the intensity of concern. "What *is* wrong with me?" She said it again, out loud, again.

In that moment she was distracted from her self-pitying and the dirt now embedded in her beautiful rug, and remembered The Cat.

"Oh my, oh…" Hearing herself speak aloud once again, she stood, an air of determination propelling her forward, and called for The Cat. The Cat did not respond. Gloria marched into the kitchen, retrieved a can of water-packed tuna from the cupboard, and opened it with the hand-held can opener. The sound would surely bring The Cat out from its hiding. Nothing. Not being the sort to coddle, Gloria set about making herself a tuna salad sandwich, layered in freshly picked Amish Deer Tongue lettuce leaves, which she thoroughly relished. The Cat would appear when The Cat appeared.

After lunch, which included a bowl of last year's slow cooked Haralson and Honey Gold applesauce, Gloria cleaned her carpeting and floors, put on her gardening shoes once again, grabbed her gardening gloves from the entryway table, and returned to the back yard. She stared at the damaged bridal wreath bush for quite some time. She could see that Hank had hosed it down and the grass along with it, leaving puddles of red-colored water to seep into the ground. The ladder was gone. Hank and his paint bucket were gone.

She stood alone with the damaged and discolored bush and went to work at salvaging whatever she could. She pulled razor-sharp pruning shears from her nearby bucket of gardening tools and began to trim away bent and broken branches. She did not want a soul to see her bush in such disarray. She thought she saw something tumble from the branch in her hand. She looked down at the ground and just at the tip of her shoe, she saw that thing that had fallen. It was not a bird's nest or egg as she had imagined. It was something instead, quite unimaginable. Gloria screamed for the third time that day. This time there was no one passing by to hear her cries or to break her fall as she passed out from sheer terror.

Perhaps it was coincidence, or luck, or the Eye of God—for Gloria was most faithful to pray that it be cast upon her and keep her safe. Most probably it was the right time of day for the mail carrier to come by with a package too large for the mailbox out front. Gloria was found when Ruth Claresman, the substitute mail carrier, went to the back of the house to deposit the package in the porch.

Ruth, recently come to live in Buffalo View Village, was betrothed to Mickey Blue Fox. They'd met in college out in Fargo where they fell in love. Ruth had never known such a love and at the age of twenty-one, that's not surprising. She felt herself daily changed by this love and eagerly anticipated the Buffalo View Village picnic when her engagement to Mickey would be announced. She daydreamed of this from sunup to sundown and was so distracted that she nearly missed seeing Mrs. Julian Stanche splayed on the ground in the most unladylike manner.

Ruth had a key to the backdoor for the purpose of leaving large packages when Mrs. Stanche was away. She dropped the package and knelt beside Gloria's body to check for a pulse as she was trained to do. She could be heard to sigh greatly when she felt a strong pulsing in both wrist and neck. Gloria stirred at the mail carrier's touch, opening her eyes to see Ruth's face far too close to her own for comfort. She promptly sat up and pushed Ruth away.

"Here," Ruth extended her arm. "Let me help you get up." Gloria shook her head trying to remember what happened but did not accept Ruth's aid.

"No, I'll be all right. Give me a minute."

"What happened? Should I call for an ambulance?"

"Don't be silly!" Mrs. Stanche growled at Ruth, then struggled to her feet. As she stood to brush soil from her gardening shirt and pants, she saw again the unimaginable thing that had fallen from the bridal wreath bush.

"It can't be," she exclaimed, now quite hysterical, and burst into tears.

A most stunned and taken aback Ruth Claresman backed away from Gloria.

"Don't move!" Mrs. Stanche's voice terrified young Ruth who stood stock still as though in a game of statue. "Don't you dare move one inch!" Mrs. Stanche pointed to an object in the path of the mail carrier's next step. Ruth screamed and jumped as far back from the thing on the ground as she could.

"I'm calling the police!" Ruth was on her phone in an instant.

Mrs. Stanche stayed put, staring at her long-dead husband's fleshy ring finger. It was still adorned with a wedding band of such unique design it could not be mistaken for or interchangeable with any other wedding band. In nine years, such a finger would be bone and barren. Mrs. Stanche fainted one more time, just as the sounds of sirens could be heard wailing on her street.

At this time, The Cat appeared, having made its way outside through the cat door at the front of the house. Unruffled by the site of Gloria's body lying flat out on the ground, it rubbed against her left leg, in that way that cats will do.

"Scat, cat!" The mail carrier attempted to shoo The Cat away for it was dangerously close to the severed ring finger at rest near Mrs. Stanche's other leg. But The Cat, an independent thinker, had spied the shiny ring, leapt over Mrs. Stanche's body, snatched the finger and fled. Just then, the sounds of screaming brakes, boots on the sidewalk, pounding on the front door, and a cry to "Open up!" from officers Franklin and Lorde was followed by "Holy Cat!" and a thud, as Detective Lorde was upended by The Cat on the run.

"You all right?" Detective Franklin asked her partner who struggled to get to his feet.

"Yeah. Damn cat!" Detective Lorde, now on his feet, brushed himself off, straightened his cap, and did his best to appear professional and dignified as Ruth Claresman rounded the side of the house to confront the officers.

"Mrs. Julian Stanche needs your help, officers!" Detective Franklin led the way to the back of the house where Mrs. Stanche's body lay. Detective Lorde, briefly distracted by the youth and beauty of the young mail carrier, nearly tripped on his feet as he followed his partner to the back of Mrs. Stanche's house for the second time that day.

"Leave me alone!" Gloria was fit to be tied over the helpfulness of Detective Franklin. "I can get up on my own two feet without your assistance!"

"Sorry, ma'am." The officer was not at all sorry but as was her way, she maintained a professionally polite demeanor whenever possible. "Didn't you faint earlier? Do you require medical assistance? I can call an ambulance."

"I do not, and you will not! What I need is my husband's finger and my husband to go with it!"

At that moment, that very moment, Julian Stanche strolled into his widowed wife's backyard. His award-winning smile, the one that got them the most beloved couple three years in a row at the Buffalo View Village picnic, knocked Gloria straight off her feet. She hit the ground hard one more time, nearly striking her head on a small mosaic steppingstone, inscribed in its center with the words, "Forever Loved" and "Bethany Lee Shifton."

Detective Lorde rushed to Gloria's aide, accompanied by Ruth Claresman, nearly done in herself with worry for Mrs. Stanche's wellbeing. Detective Franklin, an excellent patrol officer, well on her way to becoming the precinct's youngest detective, noted that Mrs. Stanche was secure in the hands of her fellow Detective Lorde. Satisfied she switched her attention to the adult, white male, age mid-forties, medium build, perhaps six foot two, a bit of gray tousled into his auburn curls, tightly cropped, brilliant blue eyes, clean shaven.

"Halt, sir! Who are you?"

Julian looked the becoming officer up and down and over before responding. "I'm here to collect what's mine."

Detective Franklin moved closer to the stranger and inquired one more time, "Who are you?"

Julian ignored her. He was intent on watching Gloria as she was helped to her feet. Julian moved closer to Gloria but was intercepted by Franklin.

"Sir! Stand away!"

Julian strolled past the officer, gave Gloria a tap on her backside, and grinning walked back from where he'd first appeared, at the side of the house. He disappeared to the wailing sounds of sirens pulling up to the front of Gloria's house. An ambulance arrived as well, to make a quick examination of Mrs. Stanche and deposit her at the emergency room of the local hospital.

CHAPTER 3
Bethany Lee

Gloria was immediately installed in an emergency room cubicle and robed in a hospital gown at the Buffalo View Village Regional Medical Center. Even though her mind was fuzzy and her vision a little off, she saw what she saw and let rip a blood-curdling scream, as faint as a summer's mid-afternoon breeze.

"Hey, Ree. You've looked better." Her presumably dead husband, Julian Stanche, was peering over her, interested more it seemed, in her bosom than her face or welfare. He reached out to touch her when she lurched for the call button at her side, to ring for a nurse, for anybody to come.

"Get out!" Her tone was meant to be harsh and mean as a military general under fire in a war zone, but she produced not much more than a squeak. A young woman, her nurse she supposed, entered her curtained cubicle with a tray of whatnots and a soothing, annoying voice.

"Now, now, Mrs. Stanche. Please calm yourself. The doctor will be here shortly." Gloria gestured wildly at her smirking, undead husband, and mouthed her complaint at his presence in her room.

"Please, Mrs. Stanche, calm yourself." The young nurse smiled at her and at Julian and at an elderly doctor who arrived in tandem with Detective Franklin, the doctor leading the way.

Franklin stood just inside the cubicle curtain while the doctor examined Mrs. Stanche.

"All's well that ends well," the doctor muttered. "You have a bump on the back of your head but everything else seems to be as it should be."

He moved his face close into hers and inquired with a foul-smelling odor of decaying lunch debris on his breath, "Are you prone to falling, Mrs. Stanche? As you know, as we age …"

Gloria abruptly stopped his nonsensical chatter with a firm grasp on his necktie. She croaked, "If you get any closer old man, I'll send you sailing through a window!"

At that, the doctor freed himself quite carefully from her grip, backed away, and looked Detective Franklin straight in the eye.

"The patient is violent?"

Julian Stanche, observing it all, burst out in a great guffaw. "Violent? Ree? Ha!" He swaggered past the doctor, the officer, and Gloria's bed with an offhand comment, "I'll be getting some coffee, but I will be back."

"Not so fast Mr. Stanche." Detective Franklin attempted to block his exit. "I have questions for you."

"Do you?"

With that, Julian brushed past Detective Franklin who promptly cuffed the man on one wrist. Julian, not one to be put down like a dog, flipped the officer off her feet. This act of aggression against an officer of the law knocked the curtains askew as the table tray tipped over and crashed to the floor. It was instinct that propelled the action, not intelligence, for there Julian stood stooped low over Detective Franklin, unable to free himself from her steady pull on his wrist as she lay flat on her back. Down, down, down. Detective Franklin brought Julian's arm down and close to her. In one smooth and swift motion, she kicked Julian's feet out from under his knees while sidling herself out of range. He hit the floor with a thud and an utterance of "Ugh!" With the hot air knocked out of him, Julian was stunned, allowing Franklin to leap onto his back and cuff the other wrist.

"As I said," Detective Franklin spoke in a huff, "I have questions for you." Franklin got back on her feet, looked down at Julian on his belly, and called for backup. "You're going downtown for some questions and to do a little cell time for assaulting an officer."

Gloria, who'd been watching the spectacle from her hospital bed, settled down with a smile on her face and closed her eyes.

"Nothing to worry about from me now, doctor." Her voice, still a whisper, was confident.

She was happy that Julian was in cuffs and about to be dragged away and tossed in a jail cell. But something nagged at her, a thought wiggling its way through the sedative that was lacing through her otherwise sharp-as-a-tack thinking. Something about the day he died. *What was it?*

The young nurse interrupted her thoughts with discharge papers. "You can go home anytime. Do you have someone who can drive you? You've got a bit of a sedative going and you shouldn't drive."

Gloria sat up and swung her legs around the side of the hospital bed, straightening her hospital gown. Her voice back to normal, she barked an order to the nurse. "Call me a cab or an Uber or whatever those pickup services are called now."

Gloria was as independent a woman as there ever was and had never needed assistance with transportation before this. But she wasn't an old woman and was sure to keep up on events and trends as required to be current should her opinion be requested at any of her social gatherings.

"We have old Charlie. He drives people to and from the hospital. He doesn't charge anything. He just likes doing it." The young nurse swept a flyaway strand of purple hair out of her face, causing Gloria to flinch with disdain. "I'll give him a call."

Unbeknown to Gloria, the driver was Charlie Boone, a long-time admirer of her mother, Bethany Lee. They'd gone to school together from first grade through their senior year. He'd always wanted to ask her on a date, but Bethany Lee was never for a minute out of her boyfriend's reach. That boy was protective, possessive, and an asshole as far as Charlie was concerned.

Everyone could tell that Bethany Lee adored the boy. Everyone knew that the boyfriend cheated on her every Wednesday night—church night—with Jillian Grove from West Silver Heights High.

Jillian was one of those fast girls. Bethany Lee was not. In the end, though, it was Bethany Lee who got pregnant by her fast-talking, handsy boyfriend who had her swooning day and night. He dumped her and the baby and never gave them another thought after he ran off with Jillian to live the high life in New York City. Turned out, Jillian's family was loaded.

Charlie helped Gloria to his car, much against her will and with protest. She yanked her arm from his proffered support.

"Slow down, girl. I knew your mamma and she wouldn't like to see this behavior on her girl."

That comment stopped Gloria in her tracks. She reacted to old Charlie's words with eyes wide and a tinge of anger mixed with disbelief in her voice. "You knew my mother? When did you know my mother?"

"We were friends since grade school." He adjusted the

rearview mirror, not giving her a sideways glance. "Let's get you in the car and at home to rest. We can talk on the way."

Gloria allowed him to ease her into the front passenger seat and watched him as he closed her car door, deft as a well-trained chauffeur. He had a jaunty gait as he walked in front of the car around to the driver's side. As he settled in beside her, she noticed that he smelled good for an old man. He smelled clean, not musty, like a lot of eighty-year-olds.

The car ride was short and quiet, the medical center being only five miles from Gloria's home. Hers was the house she grew up in, alone with her mother who never married but who always carried herself with pride and dignity. Bethany Lee was successful in real estate, making a small fortune, and left all she had to Gloria when she died six years earlier. She'd fallen in the garden, a basket of freshly cut zinnias on her arm, hit her head on the cherub fountain, and within moments of speaking her last words of gratitude to her God in Heaven, she was gone.

Gloria felt a bit unsteady because of the sedative she'd been given, but otherwise, quite clear minded. Yet she couldn't bring herself to start a conversation with Charlie about her mother, so immersed in reverie as she was. Gloria loved her mother deeply and admired everything she'd accomplished on her own. She grieved her loss every moment of every day.

Bethany Lee was perfection incarnate as far as Gloria was concerned. She tried to be the perfect daughter and rued the day she so completely failed to set a high example. It was the day she met Julian when lust revealed her true nature and goal. Her mother barely spoke to her after the wedding and up until his death. At his funeral, Bethany Lee encouraged her brokenhearted daughter to return home to grieve, while secretly rejoicing that Julian, cad that he was, was dead.

Charlie sneezed, snapping Gloria out of her daydream. She

glanced at him, not to stare, but to solidify in her mind that here was a living man who may have known her father. Bethany Lee never once revealed her father's name or why he was not present in their lives. Gloria was now intrigued and terrified to learn who her father might be, whether he also lived, where, and how far away.

For the few moments remaining of the otherwise uneventful ride to her home, Gloria forgot about her undead husband and his severed ring finger. The moment Charlie Boone pulled his car into Gloria's driveway, it hit her. That thing that had been nipping with urgency at the back of her mind rushed forward.

"Sweet Jesus," she exclaimed loud enough to be heard in the back of any amphitheater. "That man is not Julian Stanche!"

CHAPTER 4
Julian Stanche's Severed Finger

Gloria could not get into the house quickly enough to grab her phone and call Detective Franklin.

"Come in, come in," she said to Charlie, without a thank you or kindness to her tone as she attempted to exit the vehicle. In her hurry to leave the car and get inside, she forgot to unbuckle her seat restraint. The seatbelt held firm while she fumbled with the latch, almost panting with frustration.

"Let me help you with that." Charlie offered his assistance by reaching over her midsection and touching her outer thigh. She slapped him back.

"Stop that! I can do it myself. I'm not feeble. Not by years and years."

Charlie apologized while turning off the engine. He reached her car door just as she pushed it open, nearly hitting his body with full force. But Charlie was quick on his feet and backed up before the door could connect with his torso.

Gloria wobbled her way out of the car, still under the influence of the sedative she'd received in the hospital. Charlie, exhibiting kindness once more, steadied her by clasping one hand at her waist and supporting her arm with the other. This time Gloria did not rebuff the man. She wanted to tell him how much she appreciated his kindness, but she didn't. Gloria was focused on reaching Detective Franklin to tell her that the man in custody, the man who looked exactly like Julian, was a stranger.

At last in her kitchen, she gestured to Charlie with a wave of a hand toward the living room. "Please sit down. But first, if you will, remove your shoes in the entryway."

It was an automatic admonishment to strangers who were unfamiliar with her fastidious ways. But Charlie, clearly a gentleman, had already left his shoes on the rug just inside the door. As he passed by her to settle comfortably in her favorite chair, she searched for and found her phone. She punched in 911.

"Police. What's your emergency?"

"Detective Franklin has the wrong man in custody."

"Ma'am. I don't believe that's an emergency. Would you like the number to the precinct?" The dispatcher asked for her location and then provided the number.

Gloria waited with impatience for Detective Franklin to take her call. Tap. Tap. Tap. Her toes were tapping on the kitchen tile flooring while her fingers tapped on the Formica countertop. Finally, she heard the officer's voice.

"Yes, ma'am. How can I help you?"

Gloria spoke slowly with distinct determination. "You need to know, Detective Franklin that the man you have arrested, that man is not Julian Stanche."

"Yes, ma'am. Who is Julian Stanche?"

"Why, the man you arrested. But he isn't. That's not my dead husband."

"Who is your dead husband?"

Gloria was fit to be tied by this time. "Julian Stanche."

"Ma'am, if your husband is dead, why would we have him

in custody?"

Charlie, hearing the increased level of aggressiveness in Gloria's voice, entered the kitchen to stand beside her. He was quiet as a cat underfoot and scared her to jumping with a scream. She dropped the phone.

"Ma'am. Are you all right?" Detective Franklin, receiving no immediate reply, dispatched herself and Detective Lorde to Gloria Stanche's home for the fourth time that day.

"Get your hands off of me!" Gloria screeched at Charlie who was only trying to keep her from falling to the floor. His hands on her back, he gently raised her into an upright position.

"Your mother had that same fire!" Charlie chuckled and let loose of her.

Gloria bent over to retrieve her phone just as she heard sirens wailing to a stop in front of her house. "Good God. Now what?" Then she crossed herself for using the name of God in vain and sent Charlie a scathing glare. "How dare you speak of my mother in such a way!"

The pounding at her door began as Detective Franklin announced, "Police. Ma'am, do you need any help?"

"Come in, come in, but please remove your shoes." The officers entered her home but did not remove their shoes, rather covered them with blue, crime scene booties. Just as Detective Lorde was finishing up and about to set his left foot down, The Cat tore through the cat door and nearly upended the officer one more time.

"Holy Cat!" Detective Lorde exclaimed for the second time that day, as he rebalanced himself before he could crash to the floor.

Gloria's eyes were on Detective Franklin, clearly the officer in charge. "Why are you here?"

Detective Franklin exuded an air of friendliness and

authority. "We were on the phone ma'am when we were disconnected. You were talking about your husband not being dead. Julian Stanche?"

"Officers, please, come into the living room. We'll be more comfortable there."

Charlie was a quiet observer in the background, noting a struggle for power between the two women, Detective Franklin and Gloria. His money was on Gloria. Just then, there was a knock at the back door. Everyone was startled, each so highly focused on the drama unfolding before them. The room was silent but for the sound of knocking on the screen door.

"Hello! Mrs. Stanche, are you home?" Larry Grainger let himself in through the unlocked back door and hollered out a questioning hello one more time.

Mrs. Stanche was exasperated by the interruption. She rose from her position on the chair opposite Detective Franklin. "Excuse me. That's a local farmer, probably bringing eggs. I'll be right back."

Halfway through the living room, she was surprised by Grainger, shoeless, and in her house without invitation. Grainger, too, was startled, claiming he was checking on her welfare.

"What are you doing here in my house?" Mrs. Stanche was annoyed and a bit angered.

"Well," Grainger stammered, as though concocting an on-the-spot, surefire story that would explain his uninvited presence in her living room. "I … I was checking up on you. You had quite an upsetting morning and I wanted to be certain you were all right." Gloria noticed his stammer and for the first time, took notice of him.

Detective Franklin, being of astute nature, noticed Grainger's sock-clad feet and the absence of eggs or any other offering for Mrs. Stanche. The officer rose to her full height and promoted her most authoritative voice. "And who are you, sir, to Mrs. Stanche?"

Grainger, startled that Gloria was home and entertaining guests who included police officers, flushed red in the face. "I'm so sorry to interrupt.' I'll come back…"

"Sir, who are you?" Franklin took a step toward Grainger.

"Um, officer, I'm … I'm Lawrence … uh … Larry Grainger. I'm a farmer, an organic farmer." Larry, increasingly uncomfortable after having been caught where he should not have been, nearly stuttered. "I brought, I mean, I came to ask if Mrs. Stanche needed any help cleaning up after this morning's excitement, uh, trampling." He looked as though he might faint on Gloria's floral carpeting.

Detective Franklin pushed Grainger on his statement. "You said you came to check on her, to see if she was all right." Franklin took excellent notes which allowed her to repeat verbatim back to liars the holes in their stories.

Grainger was shifting from foot to foot. "I'm sorry officer. I came to help Mrs. Stanche in whatever way I could, to offer my assistance in any way I…"

Gloria interrupted. "Mister Grainger, I appreciate your interest, but I would ask that you leave now as we are attending to quite serious business." With that, she showed him to the door, stood over him as he slipped on his shoes, and firmly closed, then locked, the back door upon his exit.

I could do with a nap or a stiff drink right about now. But instead of choosing either option, she returned to the living room with urgency and addressed Detective Franklin.

"Who is the man you have in custody?"

Franklin, seated once again, responded with kindness. "I'm sorry, ma'am, I can't discuss that with you. However, I would like to know more about your husband Julian. He died nine years ago, is that correct?" Clearly Franklin had done her homework.

"His body has not yet been recovered, but he went missing after a fishing trip. A search and rescue team dragged the lake bottom but didn't find him. He was out on the boat with three friends who said he'd had too much to drink, fell overboard, without a life jacket I might add, and disappeared. He was declared dead after two years, but yes, he's been gone for nine. Gloria sat down, swept with exhaustion. "But you already know that." Detective Franklin nodded her assent.

"I thought it was Julian. I thought I was seeing his ghost. I thought he had returned from the dead when he rounded the side of my house. But then, when I saw him in the hospital, I knew that was not Julian. I did not know right away but as I observed your altercation with him, I knew something was not quite right. It came to me on the ride home with Mr. Boone, here." Gloria gestured to the old man who'd been sitting quietly, absorbing everything. "It was his finger. He had all of them."

Detective Franklin, not one to show surprise, slightly raised an eyebrow. "Your husband Julian was missing fingers?

"No. No. The bridal wreath, the blood on the bridal wreath. No, it was Hank's paint. His finger fell out of the branches. It was Julian's finger. It had his wedding band. It fell out of the bush. But it wasn't bone, it was flesh. I thought he was alive!" Gloria sighed and sat back in her chair with eyes closed. "But that wasn't Julian."

She seemed to drift away for a moment, then abruptly sat forward to challenge Detective Franklin. "Why would someone cut off Julian's finger and place it in my bush? And for that matter, where in God's name is the rest of Julian?" Gloria promptly crossed herself for the second time that day.

Detective Franklin stood to take her leave. "Mrs. Stanche, why don't you rest and we'll talk again tomorrow morning?"

Detective Lorde, who'd been silent the entire time, stood

up as well to follow his partner out of the house and back into his car. "Tomorrow," he muttered to himself. "Sure."

Gloria was too tired to care about anything Charlie may have to say about Bethany Lee or her father. "Mr. Boone, if you wouldn't mind coming another day to talk."

He smiled and raised himself from the comfortable chair, with a bit of stiffness proving his age. "Of course. I was happy to help you today and I look forward to our meeting again." His jaunty gait returned as he left Gloria's home, waving at her, and sporting a beautiful dentured smile.

Gloria felt The Cat rubbing on her leg and stooped to pick it up. "Come, come, kitty. Let's go upstairs." With The Cat purring in her arms and her focus on a much-needed nap, she did not see her husband Julian's severed finger resting on the staircase.

CHAPTER 5
Who is Morton Stanche?

While Gloria slept, Detective Franklin went about interrogating the man by the name of Stanche, but not Julian Stanche. Stanche, cuffed and processed into the Buffalo View Village jail, claimed to be Julian's twin.

"Morton. My name is Morton Stanche."

Morton spoke to Detective Franklin in a measured tone with a gleaming smile that was intended to distract her from the line of questioning she planned. But Franklin was not a femme fatale, seldom moved by the charms of just any man, certainly not one in her custody. There was only one man who caused her knees to buckle and her heart to flutter and her mind to swoon. But it was not this man. Not Morton Stanche.

"You can't keep me here, you know."

Franklin scrutinized the face of Morton Stanche – if he was indeed who he claimed to be. A search for him in the law enforcement database had yet to prove yea or nay on his claim. The name of Morton Stanche did not exist on record. Until today. No fingerprints, or birth certificate, or social security number or any other form of absolute proof of life existed for Mr. Morton

Stanche.

Morton sighed when questioned about his lack of public record identity. "We were born at home in a cabin up north with a midwife to yank us out of our mother." Morton sat forward for emphasis. "Nobody kept any records, although it may have been a Tuesday in February, if my mother could be believed, and that's not likely.

"You've never filed taxes?" Franklin appeared unruffled by his bravado.

"I've never had a job."

"How do you support yourself?" Detective Franklin barely noticed she was lured away from the question of why he appeared in Mrs. Stanche's yard earlier that day.

Morton sat back, well at ease, and flashed a magnificent smile. As his palm circled his face he snickered. "Have you seen this?" He was handsome as well as arrogant. "I've never had to work. That's what you women are for."

Franklin, always a hard worker and proud of her ability to take care of her own affairs, was infuriated. She despised gigolos and grifters. She stood abruptly, collected her papers, and left the room and left Morton to sit on his own. She needed to get a grip. *This guy is good*, she thought. *Really good.*

She was at a loss. *How do I find someone who can't be found?* Then it hit her. She could find *Julian* Stanche on record somewhere. She put an officer on the task of hunting down his records if any could be found. The birth and parental information were easy to find. He was born in Mission County, just one county over, to parents who currently reside at 124 Fairlane Avenue, in Pinecone Township. Franklin was on her feet, shouting at Lorde.

"Get moving, Lorde!" Lorde had been finishing up his lunch of fried fish and chips. "And wash that greasy stink off before you get in my car."

Detective Franklin removed Morton Stanche from the interrogation room and took him back to his cell. "You can't keep me here!" Stanche was agitated.

"You are charged with assaulting an officer, so you'll stay put until I find out what other offenses you've committed." Franklin pulled herself up to full height. At five foot, nine inches, she was no match for Stanche at six foot two, but she'd riled him, proving she was in charge.

She could still smell Lorde's greasy lunch, making the twenty-minute ride to the Stanche home a misery. With the windows wide open to clear the stench, she could hardly hear herself think. She needed to be clearheaded when she talked to Stanche's parents. *Did they have twins? What happened to Julian? What could they tell her about Morton's life? Is Morton their son's real name?*

Lorde sat brooding next to her as they drove to Pinecone Township. He was sick of her bossing him around like she was so much better than he could ever hope to be. Lorde loved women, but not the bossy types. Franklin was as bossy as they come and he had just about enough of her. Franklin knew that Lorde was incompetent and a bungler, but she needed him to witness her questioning. She did not suffer fools gladly, but she was stuck with Lorde.

"Okay, Lorde. Listen up." She was brusque and impatient.

"Listen up? You gonna deliver a State of the Union? Whaddya mean, listen up?" He glared at her. "You listen up. You talk to me like I'm some dimwit or somethin'. Knock it off!"

Franklin was surprised to learn that Lorde had a backbone. She wished he'd picked some other time to stand up for himself.

"Sorry. I was in my head." She did not turn to look his way. "Here's the deal. We are going to meet Julian Stanche's parents in Pinecone Township. The man who claims to be his twin brother,

Morton, lied about where he was born and who his mother was. We're going to find out the truth from his very-much-alive mother and father."

The rural highway was empty of other travelers. They passed farm after farm, with chickens roaming front yards and cows pasturing in the fields. The sun was strong and warm. Franklin felt herself begin to perspire from the heat, but she needed the car windows wide open to let the prairie air blow off the foul smell of Lorde's lunch.

"Jeez it's hot!" Lorde complained, started up the AC and closed the windows. Franklin wanted to smack him but after his fresh display of courage, knew she couldn't whack him. Not today.

"I'll do the questioning since I've done the research and know what I'm after. I need you to look around for evidence of the twins, maybe when they were young. I don't know exactly, but we want to be certain of who Morton is or is not by the time we leave."

"I think I know how to look around for stuff." Lorde was still in a huff.

"But we gotta be a team, so if you're still put out with me, save it for now. We'll get a beer later and sort ourselves out."

"We won't sort out much if you don't stop telling me what to do."

The detectives were quiet for the last seven minutes of the drive. Detective Franklin pulled up beside the driveway of a well-kept, small, mission-style home painted honey yellow. There was a 2016 Jeep Wrangler Sport, red, in the drive. "Did you get the license plate number?" She asked Lorde the question, well-aware he wasn't even thinking about jotting down anything. Hard to do with no notebook or pen in hand. She sighed and shook her head.

"Yeah, yeah." Lorde pulled out his notebook and wrote down the plate number. The two officers in tandem walked up the few steps to the Stanche family home. The lawn was manicured and roses were in full bloom, filling the air with a sickeningly sweet fragrance that didn't blend with the odor of fried food still lingering on Lorde. Franklin rang the doorbell.

"Who is it?" The detectives could hear a woman's voice calling out to them from somewhere in the house. "Walter, get the damn door!"

Walter Stanche, silver-haired with trim build, appeared to be in his late sixties. There was no denying that this man was the father of the man Franklin had in custody. But for the age difference, they could have been twins. "It's police, Lorinda!"

"I'm coming!"

Before Franklin could utter a word, a gorgeous, sixty-some-year-old female appeared behind Walter, pushing him aside. Her hair was cherry red and she wore an enormous diamond pendant around her neck. By the look of her dress, she was headed out for some important event or meeting.

"Officers, please, come in, come in." She was gracious and offered them a glass of lemonade or water. "I was just on my way out. But I have a few minutes. How can we help you?"

Detective Franklin introduced herself and her partner, placing emphasis on the word *detectives*. Lorde asked for lemonade and sat down on the nearest chair outside the foyer. Franklin thanked Lorinda but declined the beverage. "You are Walter and Lorinda Stanche?"

"Yes, yes. Do come in and sit." Lorinda waved them into an elegant living room, belying the modest façade of their home. "Walter, get that lemonade, would you?"

"What is this about, officers?"

"We are working an investigation that may or may not involve your son, Morton."

Lorinda was unflappable. "Morton. That boy. He's always

into something." She shook her head and smiled. "He's too good looking, you know." She looked Franklin straight in the eye and continued. "But he's never tangled with the law. So, what is this about?"

"Well, ma'am, I can't tell you about the investigation, but your son, Morton, claims to have been born by a midwife in the north country. He has no birth certificate, Social Security number, and according to him, you are deceased."

At that moment, Walter returned with Lorde's lemonade. "That boy has been spinning tales since the first day he could put a sentence together. As you can see, his mother here is vibrant and most definitely alive. As for the other details, we wouldn't know. Honestly, we haven't seen nor heard from the boy in over nine years."

"And your son, Julian?"

At that, both Walter and Lorinda flushed with emotion. "He died you know. Terrible for us. We think that's why Morton up and disappeared. Twins are so close you know. Well, you know." Walter sat down and took Lorinda's hand. "We miss him every single day and hour."

"I'm sorry for your loss." Franklin was sincere in her sympathizing. "Can you tell me how he died and where he's buried?"

Both parents looked up at her, faces awash with surprise. "We were told it was a boating accident and his body was never recovered. You know it is a terrible thing to lose a son and no grave to visit." Walter tightened his grip on Lorinda's hand.

Just then, Lorde having drained his glass of lemonade, stood and signaled he would take it to the kitchen. Walter began to object but Franklin waved him on.

Lorinda wiped her face of tears then stood and straightened herself. "If there's nothing else, officers, I am late for an appointment."

"Just one more thing, Mrs. Stanche, if you don't mind. May I have a picture of the boys together?"

Walter stood, his hand on his wife's shoulder. "Why, we don't have any. We wish now, you know, that we would have taken pictures when they were growing up. Another loss."

"Well, thank you for your time. And again, our condolences." The detectives made their way out the door and back into the car.

"You have it?" Franklin asked of Lorde. He nodded and handed her a photograph of two young boys who looked nothing at all like Morton   or   Walter   or   Lorinda   Stanche.

CHAPTER 6

Intruders

Gloria Stanche stretched lazily as she woke from her midday nap. The Cat jumped to the floor with a thud and a meow. The sunlight spilling through her bedroom window, the sound of chickadees meeping, and a slight breeze ruffling the robin's egg blue eyelet curtains made her waking feel heavenlike. All except for some child bawling down the street. Once again, she thanked the Almighty for not forcing children upon her. Momentarily she forgot about the excitement of the day. And Charlie Boone.

The image of his face woke her completely. She sat up on the edge of her bed, considering for a moment what she should do about Mr. Boone. *Do I want to know about that old man and my beautiful mother?* Gloria wasn't certain that she did want to know. On the other hand, she felt like she might want to have a casual conversation with the driver. After all, she should thank him for his kindness, and there was that chance that he knew her father. But she bristled at the very idea that she'd needed any help to begin with. The havoc of the morning played out in her mind while The Cat yowled for its supper.

Gloria glanced at the clock on her bedstand. "Four

o'clock!" Startled by the boom in her out-loud voice, she jumped up, dressed quickly, and headed downstairs to the kitchen. There on the riser in front of her, The Cat stood sniffing Julian's ring finger. Gloria stopped, gaped, then sat on the step above the offending digit. She dared herself to reach for it with hand outstretched, eyes squinting, and her head arched back in repulsion. Her forefinger and thumb twitched as they moved forward to retrieve it. She sighed. It was too much, too much for one day.

She rose from the steps and made her way into the kitchen to feed The Cat. Gloria watched the creature crouch in the way that cats do at a meal, then walked back to where the finger was dropped and picked it up. Better sense and reason allowed her to do it because she knew she had to turn it in to the authorities. To her surprise however, though the ring was real enough, the finger itself was a flexible plastic, as though from a doll or a Halloween costume. She stared at the finger while The Cat focused on its meal in the kitchen. She seated herself on the nearest chair and continued an unwavering stare.

What could be made of this? Gloria fiddled with the wedding band, wanting to slide it off the fake finger, but it was stuck, possibly with glue. She lifted the finger to examine it from every angle. There was nothing to see that would provide a clue about Julian or why anyone would leave such a ghoulish calling card in her bush.

The Cat, after a good paw and chin wash, proceeded to wander outside through the cat door. Gloria called Detective Franklin. Finding the detective away from her desk, Gloria left a message. "I have my husband's finger."

She stored the finger in a small plastic container generally used for bits of leftover coleslaw or pickles. She knew that The Cat and her own handling had likely smudged any prints, if the culprit was so stupid as to have touched the thing with his bare hands. She wondered at her readiness to think the miscreant was a man. This could be the work of a woman, but what woman and why? Julian was a philanderer. She knew he stepped out on her, as Bethany Lee said he would. But even if this was the work of a mistress, what possible motive could she have so many years after Julian's death? Maybe she was there on the boat the day he died. Maybe she wants to tell someone what she knows. *But why not just go to the police? Why such an elaborate hoax to upset me?* There were too many possible questions with no definitive answers. She decided that time would reveal the miscreant and his or her reasons for the crime.

Gloria missed Julian. For all his faults and despite her mother's warnings, Gloria's love for Julian had never faltered nor faded. He was her one, true, everlasting love. On this day, bathed in late afternoon sunlight, Gloria stood in her kitchen, holding the food container with Julian's wedding band glued to a fake finger inside, and wept. Perhaps because she'd not said goodbye or seen his waterlogged body laid in a morgue, her wounded heart never healed properly. Her mother was so unkind, so unforgiving of Gloria's love for the man. With both of her loved ones gone, she felt adrift in grief that would not abate. She was startled by the ringing of her phone.

"Hello?" Gloria's voice was cold, unfriendly.

It was Detective Franklin asking if Gloria could stop by the station with the finger.

"No, I cannot," she replied, surprised by the anger building in her tone. "I cannot do that today. You are welcome to come to my home and collect it."

She was suddenly angry as she'd never been before. It was all too much. Her bridal wreath bush was ruined. Someone horrible got into her yard and planted Julian's ring finger to terrify her. The stranger, Morton, who looked exactly like Julian had stalked her and touched her. All in all, this was a most terrible day and Gloria had quite enough of it and everyone involved. She retired to her study with a glass of wine and a garden catalog, staring without comprehension at stunning photos of Hydrangea paniculata.

It wasn't The Cat coming in the cat door that stirred her. It was someone walking about and shushing another someone in her backyard. She rose to her feet and let the all-consuming anger fill her full frame. She rounded the corner from her study to the back hallway, ripped open the backdoor, and let loose a shout that could be heard for several blocks. Neighborhood dogs began barking.

"What is going on here?" Two young boys, perhaps ten years of age, stooped behind the damaged bridal wreath bush. Gloria could see their giggling faces and hear their snorts of glee. "Come out from there! I'm calling the police!" The boys did not move a muscle, but their bodies were shaking with suppressed laughter. "And your mothers, Billy Mason and Gregory Small!"

The boys looked at one another in shock and fear and took off running, leaping, and racing through backyards. Gloria was not done with the boys or her anger just yet. "I'm calling your parents right now!" And with that, she stormed into the house, slamming the backdoor behind her. The Cat, snoozing on the sofa, was wakened by the noise. Spurred by curiosity, it made its way into the mudroom and was nearly stepped on by an enraged Gloria Stanche. It slunk under the resting bench, next to Gloria's gardening shoes, and waited out the storm.

There was no answer at either home when Gloria called the boy's parents. She left each household a scathing message, never imagining that the boys would delete them and delight in their newest prank.

Gloria brewed herself a cup of calming tea and sat to think about everything that happened that day. She made herself a small salad with a side of smoked salmon which of course, brought The Cat to her, to rub and purr against her ankles. When the dishes were done, Gloria and The Cat strolled in stride together out to the garden to rest in the early evening air. She uttered a brief prayer of thankfulness to Jesus for bringing an end to this awful day. She was a firm believer that things always looked better in the morning and thought she'd make an early night of it. But her nap and the excitement and the confusion kept her restless. She sat down inside to read after making a fresh pot of tea. An hour passed, then two. She must have dozed because it was dark when she heard a light rapping sound. The night was quiet except for the knocking at her door. Gloria froze with fear.

Get a grip on yourself, she thought. *A neighbor heard me shouting at the boys and is coming to see that everything is all right.* Gloria was about to get up and answer the door when she heard the latch loosen and the door open slowly. The hair on the back of her neck rose straight up, like she did from her chair. She bolted out the back door and screamed for help.

"Help me! Intruders!" All the dogs took up barking again. The Cat raced by her leg, escaping the uproar in its otherwise peaceful home. The nearest neighbor came out of his house with flashlight and a floodlight and hollered back at her, "What's going on here?"

"Call the police! There's a stranger breaking into my house! Call the police!"

Gloria had never been so scared or undone. She began to cry, to sob, really. Loudly. She wailed as the sound of sirens came roaring down her street. Again. But not again on the same day for it was well past midnight. No. This is another day, the next day, announcing another round of chaos and danger for Gloria Stanche.

As she stood exposed and broken by fear in her backyard garden, awaiting rescue by the police, Charlie Boone rounded the house from the front and ran to her side. "It's okay. It's all right. It was me. I was checking on you."

Gloria screamed and jumped away from Boone just as the night shift officers, Canyon and Bailey, pounded hard on the front door of her house. The neighbor, still out on his steps, waved frantically for the officers to go to the back of the house. Neither noticed his waving but heard him shouting, "In the back! In the back!" They rounded the house to the backyard to find a hysterical Gloria backing away from a man with a revolver tucked into his belt.

"Stop or we shoot!" Officers Canyon and Bailey pronounced the warning in absolute harmony to the effect they sounded like a playwright's chorus and not officers of the law about to shoot to kill. "Stop!" The musical tones were abruptly followed by a shot that rang out and set all the dogs to barking again. Gloria fell to the ground.

CHAPTER 7
CDB Loves BLW

"What the h...?" Officer Canyon shouted. Officer Bailey jumped on Boone, to protect or to capture, he wasn't sure. The Cat, having brushed the leg of Officer Canyon causing him to fire his weapon and leap into the air, bristled his back hair and with tail flared, tore off on a silent dash deep into the garden. Gloria hit the ground in a fetal crouch having had enough of fainting but still frightened witless.

Canyon surveyed the area, looking for damage from his wild-flying shot, then holstered his weapon and muttered a quiet prayer. No one hollered or yelped. That was a good sign. "What about my damned window?" The neighbor, missed by mere inches, shouted at the officers and pointed to the shattered wood frame around his front porch screen.

The officer acknowledged the neighbor with a wave and bent down to help Gloria to her feet. At his first nudging to her elbow she resisted, being quite literally frozen in place. Noticing The Cat's tail twitching from between two enormous Copenhagen Market cabbages, she began to thaw, and slapped the officer's hand away.

"Why did you shoot at him that way?" With all that happened the day before, Gloria had expanded her capacity for rage. "I'm calling the police," she barked at Officer Canyon.

"We are the police ma'am." He looked around for the thing that startled him, causing him to fire his weapon. "I'm sorry I frightened you."

"That would be my cat you're looking for." Gloria pointed to The Cat under the cabbages. "Scared of a cat? Who gave you a gun?" She stood, dusting herself off. "I thought you were trying to kill Mr. Boone!" With that, Gloria glared at Boone. "What were you doing in my house with that gun?"

Officer Bailey, at rest on old man Boone's chest, looked him straight in the eye. "What *were* you doing in the house with that gun?" Bailey cuffed him, pulled him to his feet, lifting Boone's pistol from the man's belt.

Boone turned his head toward Gloria. "Trying to protect you."

She approached Charlie with a look that made Officer Bailey flinch. "From what?" She snarled the question, nose-to-nose with him now.

"I didn't mean to frighten you." Boone relaxed as best he could with his hands cuffed behind his back. "I'm so sorry. I just meant to watch out for you, is all."

"With a gun?"

"It isn't real. The good officer here can show you that." He nodded toward Bailey who had already bagged the plastic pistol. "With all the fuss around your late husband and his twin, I thought you needed some looking after."

"What do you mean, his twin?" Gloria was caught off guard.

"His twin brother, Morton."

Gloria was shocked as she stammered, "I...I didn't know."

She wanted to sit down. She wanted to sleep. But more, she wanted answers to her ever-growing list of questions. "Officers, let Mr. Boone be. I believe he meant me no harm." Though her words were gracious, Gloria wasn't really convinced of their truth.

While Officer Bailey removed Charlie's cuffs, Gloria gave Officer Canyon the names of the boys who were meddling in her yard. "They're the ones who are most likely to have planted my husband's finger in my bush."

Officer Canyon stifled a laugh but let loose when Bailey doubled over with glee. "We're sorry," Canyon stammered, his face flushed red. "What's this about a finger then?" Both officers attempted decorum but instead, choked on escaping gales of laughter.

Gloria didn't know why the officers were laughing but she knew they were laughing at her. "Stop it! Stop it!" She yelled at them, her face burning with rage. "My husband is dead, and those boys were playing a gruesome trick on me. There is nothing funny about any of it!" And with a now stony demeanor she paused and threatened, "I will report you to Detective Franklin in the morning!"

Gloria turned her back on them to face Charlie Boone. "Please come for coffee at eleven tomorrow. I want to talk to you." Gloria walked into her garden, scooped up The Cat from under her cabbages, entered her house and locked the door behind her. "Goodnight and good riddance," she muttered, kicking off her shoes in the entry way.

As exhausted as she was, Gloria slept a fitful sleep. The neighbor's cats began caterwauling below her window as she drifted off. This caused The Cat to leap on her, then launch itself from her hip to place himself onto the reading nook lounge. From this perch, he could get the best view of the goings on below. He studied the standoff in her garden, moving his head from side to side, emitting a low growl. Gloria emitted a mild curse, then a sigh. When the morning light spilled into her room, she was amazed that she had slept at all.

Charlie Boone was prompt. Gloria expected nothing less from the old man. As she prepared the coffee setting and arranged shortbreads and miniature orange muffins on a tray, she could think of nothing but her father. Bethany Lee thought little of men and their contributions to the lives of women. Gloria easily assumed that her mother's distaste for men had everything to do with the man who'd fathered her daughter. She'd always imagined he was a scoundrel. And though Julian earned and deserved every disdainful look and criticism Bethany Lee sent his way, Gloria believed that Julian was the foil for her father, a black-hearted cad. She was certain of it.

It came as no surprise, but with a sickening feeling, that Gloria learned her father was as bad and terrible as she'd imagined him to be.

"It broke my heart," Charlie said, "every time he went out on her. And then when he deserted her with you on the way, it took all my will not to hunt him down and do him in."

Charlie sipped his coffee after adding a bit of milk. He was meticulous in his handling of the wrapper on the muffin. Gloria could see that he enjoyed the two bites he took to devour it before reaching for another.

"Would you like more coffee?" She didn't want to leave her chair or interrupt his story but her hostess duties would come first.

"If it's no trouble." He wiped his face carefully, then tucked his napkin under the edge of his luncheon plate. "That was a delicious muffin! You are quite the accomplished woman, are you not?"

His praise did not move her. She refreshed his cup,

removed his plate and napkin, and urged him to continue.

"I am sorry girl, to be telling you this, but you should know the courage and fortitude of your mother. When we were young, she dazzled me. She still does."

"The two of you were involved?"

"Oh, not in the way you're thinking. Your mother had eyes and heart for Jerry Trout, and only Jerry Trout." Charlie paused, thinking. "Your father …," Charlie paused again, "your father was a lying, cheating, bastard. It broke my heart to see how he treated Bethany Lee." Charlie pulled a handkerchief from his pants pocket and wiped his nose. "I loved her. Always loved her. And I protected her. The same way I will protect you if need be." He was sweet and sincere and earnest.

"I don't need your protection, Mr. Boone. I've been fine on my own these last six years and I'll be fine on my own in the future."

Charlie smiled at her in a warm, fatherly way. "I don't doubt that. But indulge me. You've had quite the upset and honestly, it looks like your past has come back to bring you trouble. I'd like to help, if you need me, whenever you might need me."

Gloria found herself appreciating his sincerity. She had forgotten about Morton Stanche. She had forgotten for a moment about Julian. But she hadn't forgotten that Boone was in her house at night with a gun. Gloria stood over the old man, coffee pot in hand, giving him her most fierce and determined look.

"Why were you in my house last night while I was sleeping and how did you get in here?"

Charlie looked at her with eyes of innocent surprise. "Why, I told you why I was here. And I still have a key. I cared for your mother's home and garden when she was away traveling."

"I'd like to have that key now, Mr. Boone." Gloria turned

her back on Boone to return the coffee pot to its warming plate. When she turned back to face him, he had risen from his chair. The house key was on the table. She picked up the key and put it in her pants pocket.

"I'm sorry if I've upset you. It's just, there are things you don't know …" He noticed her fine form and beautiful face and features. It's just that … you look so much like your mother."

"Yes. I am well aware of how I look, Mr. Boone."

"I know that I must seem a silly old man to you."

Gloria resisted his attempts to charm her. She did not trust him, despite his long-standing relationship with her mother. "No, not a silly old man. A wily old man. I don't trust you or your motives."

"Fair enough. But know this. Your husband and his brother were long in cahoots. They gained knowledge of your mother's financial wellbeing." Boone lifted an eyebrow and pushed his face forward to emphasize his statement.

"The boys were shifty and greedy and licentious as anyone. And charmers. Julian married you for your mother's wealth." Seeing the look of pain on Gloria's face, Boone reached out as if he could comfort her after saying such a horrible thing about the man she'd loved all her life. "I'm truly sorry."

Gloria, stunned, could not object or stop listening to Boone's goings-on. She was desperate for him to stop talking. Her heart was melting. Tears were forming. She felt weak in the knees. But he kept talking.

"Have you ever wondered why Julian's body was never found?"

This was too much for Gloria. "Please, stop. Just stop!" She waved her hand at the old man, gesturing him to the door.

"I will leave but know that I will be watching out for you. I loved your mother more than I can ever say. She was betrayed by love. You have the same heart, steadfast and loyal. I beg you to think of what I've said." Eyes downcast, he finished. "There is more to tell."

Gloria, crestfallen and disheartened, shifted her gaze away from Boone. "Go."

She watched the back of him walk away, through her door, to his car. The Cat was at ease on the warm hood and refused to budge. Boone picked up The Cat, set it on its feet and stroked its ears. Charlie watched The Cat mosey across the driveway, out of harm's way. As he drove off, Charlie looked back at Gloria's house and smiled.

Could things get any worse? Gloria needed to think or sleep. She wasn't sure which she needed more. She walked into the garden, taking a seat on the bench by her mother's fountain. There she cried and then she sobbed. At which moment her suitor, Larry Grainger, arrived with a flat of red and white stripped petunias for her hanging baskets. And an apology.

CHAPTER 8
Gloria's Great Truth.

Larry set a flat of petunias down on the sidewalk as Gloria lifted a handkerchief to her eyes, dabbing away her tears. "Gloria, what is wrong? Can I help?" He spoke in gentle tones as he approached her.

Gloria slid to the far side of her bench, holding out her hand to signal he should stop from coming too close. "What are you doing here?"

Grainger ignored her warning and continued his advance. "I brought the petunias you asked for." He turned his head toward the flat of flowers. "I thought they might cheer you and distract from your recent disturbances and troubles."

Gloria rose to face him, commanding him to stop. "Stay where you are, Larry Grainger!" You were in my house without invitation." She clasped her phone and prepared to call the police. "Why? And don't you dare lie to me!"

Larry stayed put. "I'm sorry. I apologized and I am here to apologize once again. The door was not locked and when you didn't respond to my knock, I let myself in to check on you."

"Tell the truth or so help me, I will prosecute you for

trespassing." Gloria's face hardened with rage.

"I am telling you the truth!" Grainger was adamant and did not back down or away. "Gloria," his eyes downcast, he spoke just above a mumble, "I'm in love with you." He lifted his eyes to look into hers. "And so, I worry. Ever since your mother passed, leaving you here alone, I worry about you."

She glared at him, sizzling. "If you think that I'd accept your flirtatious bait instead of the truth, then you can leave and never come back. And take that flat of petunias with you when you go," she took a step toward him as though she might slap him in the face, "or I will call the police!"

Grainger did not protest but tipped his sunhat to Gloria as he skirted the gifted flat of petunias. His arrogance was astounding and furthered her suspicions that he was up to no good where she was concerned. Alone again in her garden, with the sound of his farmer's truck driving off, Gloria considered all that had transpired yesterday. She looked at her phone for a moment, then called Detective Franklin.

"Detective Franklin, this is Gloria Stanche. I have my husband's wedding ring. Now I want his finger and the rest of him. I believe his brother Morton had the ring all along and set up those boys to plant it in my bridal wreath bush. I don't know how, and I don't know why. But I believe Larry Grainger is in on it with Morton."

Detective Franklin listened without interruption. "And I cannot figure out why there was blood on my bridal wreath bush. There was blood on it before Hank Broden spilled his paint bucket. Did you test it? Whose blood is it? I am overrun with suspicious characters and evidence that reads to me like there is a criminal coverup in process or perhaps a plot is building against me. I am quite afraid."

Within three minutes, sirens could be heard wailing down

Gloria's street. Four squad cars and a forensics team swarmed her back yard before she could muster herself off the garden bench. Franklin approached Gloria.

"We can sit over there." She rose and pointed to a pair of ironwork chairs near her mother's cherub fountain, bubbling faithfully, lending an air of calm to this terrible moment.

"You've had a lot of trouble in the last day. I'm sorry that you've been put in this position." Franklin's tone was soothing and her manner sincere. "We still have quite a lot to talk about, don't we?"

Gloria nodded in assent. "I want to know where my husband is." There was such a sadness in her voice. Her shoulders sloped a bit as she turned her face away from Franklin and toward her mother's cherub fountain. She straightened and gave Franklin a piercing look. "Did you call the parents of those boys? The officers that were here last night were useless and fools and more trouble than they were worth."

Franklin took notes as Gloria spoke. "What did happen last night, Mrs. Stanche?"

She recounted her awful fright and ensuing disappointment and disgust with the boys hiding in her bridal wreath bush. But it was the visit by Mr. Boone that had her the most unnerved and distrustful. "Who is he to insert himself this way, and in the middle of the night, entering my house without invitation? I believe he is a liar and I wonder now if he has anything to do with the appearance of my husband's wedding ring."

"He met with us yesterday, correct?"

"Yes. And Mr. Grainger, the man who walked in on us, I believe he's involved as well."

"You believe, Mrs. Stanche, that Mr. Boone and Mr. Grainger and Mr. Morton Stanche are in cahoots."

"What else could it be?"

Gloria could not arrive at a unifying theory for the unexpected presence of all three men at the same time in her yard and garden and home and hospital room.

"I met Mr. Boone at the hospital when I needed a driver to take me home. As you know, he volunteers. He couldn't have known I would be next on his delivery list."

"It seems unlikely, Mrs. Stanche. He knew your mother well, correct?"

Gloria threw up her hands and interrupted. "Detective Franklin, what about my husband's decoy finger? Where is Julian? Isn't that where we should begin this investigation? All the rest looks like a healthy pile of red herrings to me!" She was furious, not at Detective Franklin who was doing her job surely, but at everyone else and about everything that was happening to her.

"I honestly don't care about those men. Well, I do. They shouldn't be showing up on my property at all hours. But I deeply care about the remains of my husband." There was the truth of it. "I deeply care."

Just then, Hank Broden rounded the house to the back and walked straight away into one of the forensics officers. The officer's yelp was heard for at least three blocks.

"Jesu…" He stopped himself short in as he flailed his arms, fighting with himself to keep balance. At that moment, The Cat made a dash from beneath the bridal wreath bush that had been under examination. The teetering officer's back left foot settled with his full weight on The Cat's tail. The Cat in full screech furthered the toppling. The officer would have landed on his back on the ground if Hank Broden hadn't been quick to grab his arms and pull him forward. Broden was small and stocky. The officer was tall and lanky. Together they balanced each other, until they didn't. The Cat was long gone.

Gloria burst. The tears would not stop. "My cat! Where is

my cat?" She sobbed and cried. It was all too much. She could no longer pretend that the turbulent events of the last two days hadn't exposed her every need and longing to feel safe and certain and loved. Her wounded cat, scared and lost somewhere in the garden, underscored her pain. "I must find him."

Gloria called for The Cat who wouldn't come. She dried her eyes, her back to the investigative team, then turned to face Detective Franklin.

"As long as Julian's body is missing, I have hope that he will come back. Whatever he's been doing will have brought him to his senses and home. His wedding ring does not prove he's dead. It proves to me that maybe, maybe he was trying to return and was prevented from doing so, most likely by Morton."

"I will make it my first priority to uncover, once and for all, exactly what happened to your husband. My team will investigate other aspects of this case and will report to me, but I assure you that I agree. Your husband's whereabouts, alive or dead, begs a thorough investigation."

Gloria spotted The Cat settling down under a lilac bush, a freshly captured mouse in its jaws. She studied the bubbling fountain and listened to its gentle gurgle. "Thank you, Detective Franklin. Thank you."

"I would suggest however that you invite someone to stay with you until we figure out what's going on and that you replace all the locks in your house and install—immediately install—a security system."

"I will do no such thing, Detective Franklin." Gloria stood firm on her own ground as an independent woman who could manage through even these extraordinary circumstances.

Just then, Lucille Persons arrived in Gloria's back yard, carrying a gift basket of freshly-baked muffins. She stopped in her tracks, struck by all the commotion around Gloria's bridal wreath bush. Hank Broden was getting to his feet and the officer he'd knocked over was up and well away from the handyman. One of the team shouted out to Detective Franklin, "There isn't any blood here."

Franklin looked inquisitively at Gloria. "Well, I did try to clean my bush with soap and water so I may have removed the evidence." Gloria frowned. "I suppose I washed away evidence."

"Wait! We've found something!" The officer was shouting again. Franklin left Gloria's side to see what the team had uncovered.

"Mrs. Stanche," Lucille Persons, still standing in the same spot, also shouted out. "Is it all right for me to enter?"

Gloria, unaware that Lucille was in her backyard, studied her for a moment then waved her in and over to the bench. "Yes. Yes." Lucille nearly tripped over the forgotten flat of petunias.

Gloria noticed Hank Broden standing near the officers and called out. "Hank. Come here." Hank didn't move a muscle or twitch. "Hank!" She barked his name.

At that, Hank Broden turned his head toward Gloria and pointed back toward her bridal wreath bush. The team stood back from Franklin as she squatted to inspect something on the ground.

Gloria stood, ignoring, Lucille, and made her way to Broden to find out what had him stuck in place and pointing. Lucille set the basket of muffins on the ironwork table between the chairs, next to the bubbling fountain, and peered at Hank and Gloria and Detective Franklin as they all stooped down in unison to inspect something that she could not make out.

"Sherman!" Franklin shouted to one of her forensic officers. "How in hell did you all miss THIS?"

CHAPTER 9
Bones

Hank Broden took a step back as Officer Sherman approached. Sherman knelt down to look closely at what Franklin was shouting about. With great care, he lifted a pile of bones from a hand that had long ago lost its flesh and function and bagged them for later analysis.

Lucille Persons sat down in shock at what she witnessed. To her credit, Gloria did not faint or swoon. She stood and announced to Detective Franklin that the bones likely belonged to her husband Julian.

"And how would you know that?" Franklin inquired.

"I don't know that, but I don't doubt it." She turned to walk away, before she could shed a tear. Gloria could smell the luscious scents steaming from Lucille's gift basket of muffins. She felt real hunger for the first time in two days. As she ravaged a cranberry muffin, Lucille Persons put her arm around her beloved and smiled.

"I'm here for you, Gloria, whatever you need."

Gloria nodded in thanks. Her mouth was so full of muffin she could not speak. She looked back over her shoulder to watch the officers finish up when she spotted Hank Broden slinking away. "Wait!" She shouted at Broden but couldn't get his name out until she swallowed what was left of the muffin in her mouth. "Hank!"

Hank turned to look at her contorted face and stopped. Gloria stood up and called him to her. When he was near enough, she asked, "Why are you here?"

"Yes, ma'am. I come to ask ye when ye'd want me to finish up the trim work." He pointed to the dormers where he'd been applying red paint when he fell off his ladder.

"Oh, well, I can't think about that right now." Gloria fought back tears.

"Yes, ma'am." Hank Broden tipped his hat and ambled away.

Gloria turned her attention to Lucille. "I appreciate that you stopped by." Gloria sighed a sigh of the doomed. "I was hungry." She sniffed the air, fully scented with the aroma of baked goods. "I'm not myself."

As she reached for another muffin, Lucille clasped Gloria's hand in her own, preventing her from achieving what appeared to be a lemon poppy seed variety.

"I'm here for you, Gloria. I want you to know that." Her sincerity was clear as she gazed into Gloria's eyes. Gloria, no stranger to flirtatious gazes, pulled her hand away, grasping a muffin and standing in one smooth motion.

"I appreciate that, Mrs. Persons. And I thank you for the muffins. It's kind of you. But I need time to myself, so if you wouldn't mind, I'm going in the house now." She called for The Cat who had finished with all but the tail of the mouse.

Lucille was crestfallen. "I understand. I do. I just want you to know…"

Gloria interrupted her. "Again, thank you." She took firm

hold of the basket and walked with The Cat to the back door, entering without a glance toward the officers scavenging in her bush. She didn't dare look but listened over the din for the sounds of Lucille Person's leaving. Satisfied that she was gone, Gloria sat down on her entryway bench and burst into tears. The Cat settled down to clean itself from any remains of mouse while Gloria tried unsuccessfully to compose herself, wiping tears away with her sleeve. She couldn't remember a time when she had been so short of manners or so publicly free with her emotions.

Just as she readied herself to enter the main house, she heard a knock at the entryway door. The Cat, skittish from all the activity of late, dashed into the house and presumably up the stairs. Gloria sighed. *Good God. What now?* And then she crossed herself. She opened the front door to find Detective Franklin.

"I've sent my team off. I'd like to finish our talk if that's all right with you."

Gloria gaped at the detective, her cheeks still wet with tears. "I don't know what I can say."

"That's all right, I'll ask questions and you can do your best to answer them."

"But I really don't feel up to it right now. The bones and all. In my yard. The bones."

"I understand. I won't take up much more of your time."

With that, Gloria let Franklin into her home again. "Please remove your shoes." The request was made of Detective Franklin as Gloria herself slipped into her house shoes, leaving those she'd worn in the garden on a welcome mat beside the entry door. Franklin followed suit and kept a respectful distance from Gloria as she led the officer into the living room once again.

Gloria did not offer coffee or tea or lemonade or any of the muffins from Mrs. Persons' basket, which she deposited on the kitchen counter on her way through to the living room. Gloria's countenance was grim. "It's all too much, you know."

Detective Franklin was supportive and encouraging. "Yes, it's a lot, Mrs. Stanche. I understand. But think of it this way. We will discover what happened to your husband. I fully support your suspicions that something is happening around his death even though he has been gone for such a long time.

Gloria closed her eyes and forced herself to hold back more tears. She felt that she might cry for eternity and even that might not be long enough to expunge her grief. "I don't understand any of this, but I know one thing. I must get hold of myself."

Detective Franklin nodded. "I want you to know that the bones have been removed with as little disturbance to the surrounding area as possible, but there is damage that could not be helped. My officers also found a few broken branches with what appears to be blood. As soon as I can update you, I will."

"Thank you, officer. Is there anything I can do to help?"

Franklin smiled. "There is. I'm wondering if you have anything of your husband's that we might use in determining if there is a DNA match to the bones we found." Franklin continued, "And if you would keep an eye out and an ear turned to anything that you feel is out of step with your normal day-to-day."

"Detective Franklin," Gloria stood, indicating she was ready to end this interview. "I will let you know if I come up with something. Right now, I need some time alone. If you wouldn't mind leaving."

Gloria's stony expression indicated to Franklin that she would get no more from Mrs. Stanche today. "Certainly. Please get back to me as soon as you can with whatever you may find, if anything."

Just then The Cat wandered into the living room and plunked itself down in a sunny patch on the carpeting, stretched out full body, and closed its eyes for a mid-morning nap. Gloria stared at The Cat for the longest time, longing to feel so at peace, to rest with ease.

"Detective Franklin, I don't know if you realize this, but there is no one I can talk to about my suspicions. You are the only one who can investigate my questions and perhaps provide answers. There's no one else I can trust. I'm even suspicious of the handyman, whose done nothing but bumble us all into this series of mysterious events."

Franklin acknowledged Gloria's concerns. "Again, a lot has transpired in a short period of time around something that happened many years ago. I will get to the bottom of this, and I will inform you of my progress as much as I am able." Detective Franklin put her notebook away and thanked Mrs. Stanche for being so cooperative. "I'll be in touch."

Gloria stood still in the living room watching The Cat and waiting for the sound of Detective Franklin's car pulling away from her home. She closed her eyes, breathed in deeply, then with great determination marched up the stairs to sort through her memory box of cherished mementos, including a few of Julian.

Brilliant sunlight and radiating heat shocked Gloria as she entered her bedroom. She had forgotten that it was summer. She felt cold, the kind of cold that no wool wrap or cable-knit sweater would warm. The Cat leapt on the bed and selected the sunniest, hottest spot on her coverlet to settle in for a thorough wash and a nap.

The memory box, untouched for nine years but for dusting, seemed smaller than she remembered. Gloria reached up to the top shelf of her closet to slide the box toward her and to guide it gently into her arms. Her stomach churned just enough to set loose her mother's haranguing voice. *He's no good! You have to know that! How many women, how many times? When will you put an end to this ridiculous marriage?* Gloria closed her eyes and willed the voice in her head to stop. Then an image of Julian arose, his arms outstretched to her, his words promising her the world. She felt sick and shivered.

She sat in the bedroom reading chair. The streaming sunshine stroked her cheek as she lifted the lid from the box. She pulled an old toothbrush wrapped in plastic out from beneath a stack of photographs. She'd saved it on the off chance that there might be cause for a paternity test from one of his women. *How will I explain this to Detective Franklin without making myself appear pathetic?* Every bad thing her mother had scolded her about was true of her marriage. She knew that. *I thought there would be a child, not a murder, and certainly not this mess.*

Gloria put the box back in the closet but left the toothbrush on her nightstand. This piqued The Cat's curiosity. Gloria glared at The Cat. "Don't you dare!" The Cat was more interested in staying put than pouncing on the plastic-wrapped toothbrush. Gloria snatched it off the nightstand and headed downstairs to call Detective Franklin and make a cup of soothing tea. On her way down the steps, the front entry doorbell rang. She sighed, sat down, and waited for the visitor to go away. But the caller was insistent and was now, pounding on the door.

"I'm coming," she mumbled as she passed through the living room. Glancing through the window she could see Morton Stanche, his hand raised to begin pounding again. Gloria tucked the toothbrush in her shirt, pulled out her phone, and called the police. She didn't care who arrived.

Morton fidgeted at the door, shuffling his feet, peering through the window. She held her breath when The Cat ran past her and into the living room. But Morton did not react to the movement, if in fact he saw The Cat at all. And as the sound of sirens roared toward her house, she watched Morton race to his car and flee.

She was about to stand up from her perch on the stairway when the doorbell rang again. Gloria could see Ruth Clarendon holding a small package for delivery. Ruth appeared nervous and hesitant as she addressed Gloria with a good morning, lifting the package toward her. With a sudden and hasty look over her shoulder toward the approaching police officers, she fumbled the package and dropped it to the ground.

"Oh, I'm sorry!" Ruth bent over to retrieve the package as officers appeared, leapt from their squad car, and pulled their guns, aiming at Ruth's backside and ordered her to stand up and show her hands. Just then, The Cat, disturbed by more commotion, raced past Gloria's legs, past Ruth's frightened form, and straight between the feet of the patrol officers causing one to trip and tip and fire his weapon.

The bullet went wild and as good fortune would have it, hit no one. But like a magnet to disaster, the same neighbor's house was hit again. While he relaxed in an oversized wicker chair with green and gold striped cushions that Gloria admired, the bullet slammed into the front porch eave. Upon hearing the sirens, the neighbor had considered whether he should stay to watch whatever drama would unfold or scurry inside for protection.

"Hey!" He shouted out and disappeared inside his house while Ruth collapsed on Gloria's front step, reduced to panic and sobbing.

"Oh, you poor thing!" Gloria reached out to help her to her feet when the second officer, still poised to shoot, commanded her to stop.

"Are all of you incompetent?" Gloria was fearless in her rebuke. "Shooting at a small cat and threatening our postal carrier. It's unforgiveable!"

Detective Franklin arrived, assessed the situation before stopping her car in the street. "Stand down, officers!" Her order could be heard as far as four blocks away, for it was a quiet, calm morning that bode no warning of mayhem. Franklin left her car to order the two officers back to the station.

"I'll deal with you later." She tried to calm Ruth and settle Gloria down, but they were both so hotly wired she couldn't manage either one. "Can we go inside and talk about what just happened?"

Gloria took hold of Ruth's hand. "Come in with me." Together, the one shaken, the other furious, they walked into Gloria's home, removing their shoes in the entry, forgetting entirely about the package   Ruth   delivered.

CHAPTER 10
Bethany Lee

"I've thought so all along." Detective Franklin sat back in her desk chair at the 2nd Precinct building in the heart of Buffalo View Village.

No one knew why the building had 2nd Precinct carved into stone above the main entrance. Mr. Thomas Littlehorn should know, being the village historian, but he did not. In his annual village historical celebration oratory, he would offer a theory.

"There was speculation that when the 1820s military outpost was demolished to make way for peace in the community, that perhaps it was the first law and order establishment preceding the incorporation of the village. Others speculated that was unlikely since there was never such an unruly crowd as the troops that occupied Buffalo Ridge Fort."

But today Littlehorn was meeting with Detective Franklin in her 2nd Precinct office on an entirely different research topic.

"I have some papers here that support my notion that Julian Stanche was in a real estate deal with Bethany Lee Shifton." Littlehorn shared the information with a proper degree of gravity. After all, he was surely helping to expose some long-hidden crimes, misdemeanors, and important criminals.

Detective Franklin met with Mr. Littlehorn earlier in the day, requesting discretion and some digging into village records that may shed light on the disappearance of Julian Stanche. The documents Littlehorn uncovered were dated from ten years prior and revealed plans for a partnership between Shifton and Stanche in the construction of a visitor center at the edge of the village. The partnership agreement was signed and dated by both parties. Included in the file were blueprints and surveyor's notes and comments. In addition, there was a purchase agreement between the county and S&S Real Estate Development LLC for the required plot of land. However, the county had no record of title transfer for the property nor record of cash paid in a healthy sum of $750,000.

"I was certain there was relationship between the two. Now you've confirmed it! Thanks, Tom."

"Sure. Do you want me to bring over the packet?"

"No, no. I'll pick it up from you. And keep this to yourself, will you?"

"Sure thing, June." Thomas Littlehorn was not only the village historian, but he was also Detective Franklin's fourth grade math teacher. To him, she would always be an eleven-year-old named June, although he often praised her achievements as an adult.

Detective Lorde looked up from his desk as Franklin was preparing to leave. "You need me to come along?"

"No, thanks. I'm going to grab some lunch. Have you learned anything more about Boone?" Lorde grumbled an inaudible response. "Well, keep at it. There's something there."

Lorde detested playing second to Franklin and would keep whatever he found on Boone, if anything, to himself. But his interest was not on his partner's agenda. He was far more interested in the Reverend's wife. What was she doing at Stanche's house anyway? Was she really just passing by? Yes, that was the excuse he needed to pay her a visit, officially, of course.

Detective Lorde, or "Lusty" as he was known about town, hadn't been able to get the image of Lucille's tempting cleavage out of his mind. He was an attractive enough man and impeccably groomed, even if he was a bungler and a bit of a dolt. Women were drawn to him. He seemed like a man who needed care and attention, a lost little lamb who'd look good on any girl's arm. He knew it and used this charm to lure even the most reluctant of prey.

He suspected that Lucille would present a challenge, being married, and to a reverend no less. Lorde could read a woman and this woman read like a romance novel. She was ripe for seduction. Lorde's vanity would not allow him to know or suspect that Lucille Persons would never be interested in a man like him. Or any man, ever again.

Since meeting Gloria Stanche at a garden club gathering seventeen months prior, Lucille Persons' world had been turned inside out. Gloria dazzled her and she could not think of much else other than how to be at Gloria's side as often as possible without revealing her secret passion for the widowed Mrs. Stanche.

Detective Lorde sat in his car parked in front of Lucille's home. The reverend had just left the house and was on foot, walking toward the church, two blocks over. Lorde waited until the coast was clear and made his way to Lucille's front door.

"Oh, Officer!" Lucille was taken off guard by the appearance of Detective Lorde at her door. "Is this about Mrs. Stanche?" She blushed a little as her beloved's name rolled from her lips. He was emboldened by her obvious pleasure at his arrival.

"May I come in?"

"Certainly, officer. How can I help you?"

Lucille, with a sweeping gesture, led Detective Lorde into a bright enclosed porch, where she had been sipping morning tea and reading. Lorde brushed by her, grazing her upper arm, and mumbled a disingenuous apology. His skin tingled from contact as he took a seat well within reach of her.

"Mrs. Persons," he began, "how well do you know Mrs. Stanche?"

"Not that well, actually. We met at garden club last year." Lucille squirmed in her chair; her face still flushed. "Where are my manners? Can I get you some coffee or tea?" Lucille stood to leave the room before Lorde could answer.

In the kitchen, Lucille tried to compose herself. *This is ridiculous!* She scolded herself but the scolding did nothing to calm her beating heart. *Get hold of yourself!* At that she set a pot of coffee to brew, drank a full glass of water in one gulp, brushed a stray hair away from her forehead, and returned to face the officer.

"The coffee will be ready in a moment."

Lorde nodded and thanked her. They were both distracted for a moment by the noise from three boys playing football in the street. Of course, their ball hit the side of Detective Lorde's car, setting off an alarm that could be heard for a mile on this calm day. Lorde rushed outside to confront the boys who scattered in four directions, one being confused at which way to go, so tried two options.

Lorde's hesitancy gave him a chance at that boy, but the officer was clumsy and the boy was quick. Lorde muttered a string of expletives, then checked his car for damage. The offending football rested in all innocence by the right front tire. Lorde kicked it up the curb, jabbing his toe into the concrete. He saw stars and uttered additional expletives. Just then, the Episcopal minister arrived at his home, apparently having forgotten one thing or another.

"Are you all right sir?" He asked after Lorde's wellbeing.

Lorde snarled at him, got in his car, and headed back to the precinct office.

~~~~~

"Thomas," Detective Franklin greeted Thomas Littlehorn at his modest home. "Thank you for seeing me again today."

"June, I'm quite intrigued with this case you're on. It smacks of trouble that's been simmering for years."

Franklin nodded in agreement. "Yes. It does. What I'm really after right now is the body of Julian Stanche. The insurance company was satisfied that he died in a boating accident though his body was never found."

"I recall that case. And I think there is something here to be uncovered. The S&S Development partnership seems to be fraudulent since the land deal exchanged funds but no land. And I wonder who received the $750,000 payment and from whom and for what? It certainly was not land. A deadly boating accident that yields no body is equally questionable."

The two sat at Littlehorn's old Formica-top kitchen table. Littlehorn provided ham sandwiches on rye bread with a tray of mustards and mayonnaise. A pitcher of lemonade and two empty glass tumblers were placed in the middle of the table. Franklin carefully moved them aside, thanked Littlehorn for lunch, and pulled the partnership documents from a large manilla envelope. She took a bite of her sandwich, then another, unconscious of consuming any of it as her concentration was laser-focused on the 15 pages of documents.

Littlehorn remained quiet while Franklin studied the pages in front of her. He could hear a car alarm sounding what seemed a few blocks away. Franklin did not notice. When she had read and re-read the contents of the manila envelope, she sat back and stared at Littlehorn.

"Oh, my God!" She exclaimed. At that, Littlehorn smiled and cleared the table. Franklin sat up straight in her chair, shuffling two pages back and forth, over and over. "Are you sure?"

"In this world, June, we can be sure of nothing, but it certainly appears to be true."

~~~~~

Returning to the precinct office, Franklin's mind was on fire. She now had nearly irrefutable proof of Morton Stanche's involvement but no clue as to how exactly he fit into the puzzle of corruption and possible murder. Were they lovers, Bethany Lee, and Morton? Did Morton disappear with the mysterious land deal cash? And why is he in Buffalo View Village? Maybe he's looking for the cash and thinks Gloria Stanche has it hidden somewhere. At the next light, Franklin turned away from the precinct building and headed for the highway, back to Mission County and another visit to Walter and Lorinda Stanche's home.

"I've been called away on another matter." Franklin placed a call to Lorde. "Did you find anything new on Morton Stanche?"

Lorde was caught up in paperwork about damage to his car and hadn't given a thought to Morton Stanche. He clicked off, muttered and sputtered, and limped a little on his way to the Captain's office with his report.

Franklin raised an eyebrow in surprise at the abrupt end to their call and redialed, only to be sent directly to voicemail. She shook her head and clicked off.

"Useless!" Franklin sat a little straighter in her seat and with pursed lips, kept driving. When she turned on to the Stanche's street, she slowed down and parked at the corner. She watched as Walter, Lorinda, and Morton carried luggage from the house and packed the Jeep. They appeared to be arguing but Franklin could not hear what they had to say.

As Lorinda and Walter climbed into the Jeep, Morton stepped into his car parked directly behind them. Franklin revved her engine. With siren blaring, she sped forward in an attempt to block the vehicles from behind.

Morton saw her and hit the gas. In reverse, tires squealing, he backed up and rammed the passenger front side of Franklin's squad. Franklin was out of her car in an instant and at Morton's door before he could switch gears to escape. With her weapon drawn and pointed at Morton's chest, she ordered him to halt. He sped past her. Franklin fired. About a half a block away, his front left tire flattened by Franklin's marksmanship, he was dead in his tracks.

"Move, twitch, or think, and this gun takes off your head!" Franklin's weapon was now aimed directly at Morton's temple. He looked at her with a look that could shoot back. Then he grinned, a most gorgeous and disarming grin. Lorinda and Walter were long gone.

CHAPTER 11
Ian McDougall

Morton's grin put Franklin off guard for as long as it took him to slam his door into her midsection. Her gun went off sending a shot wild. Franklin, knocked over and winded, tried to shoot at Morton again but loosed her grip on the weapon as he lodged his full bodyweight onto her hand.

"Hey," shouted the next-door neighbor who had walked out of his house and onto his front porch to investigate the commotion. Ignoring the ongoing street battle between the downed officer and Morton Stanche, he complained, "Who's gonna fix this?" He pointed to a shattered porch door frame where the wild shot hit.

Just then, spilling from their homes, came neighbors to the aid and defense of Franklin. While the complaining neighbor looked on, the horde of locals swarmed Morton's car preventing him from any further attempt to escape. A young man, perhaps eighteen or so, stooped over Franklin and offered to help her to her feet. Shaken and sore, Franklin accepted his help but reached out her broken hand and yelped in pain when she made contact.

Anyone who may have been paying close attention would have seen Detective Franklin fight back tears. "My gun," she said to the young man, "please hand me my gun."

Just then, a siren could be heard coming their way. The neighbors parted like the Red Sea at God's command, making a certain path for the oncoming ambulance. Two Mission County Sheriff's vehicles pulled up from the opposite direction, bringing four officers to investigate the call they'd received as shots fired.

"Hey, you!" The disgruntled neighbor shouted at the officers, "What about me?" But he couldn't be heard above the clamoring of the crowd, avid and eager to help the investigation.

Mission County Sheriff, Ian McDougall, took Franklin's pistol from the young man, giving him an appreciative eye. "Thank you. Please go to Officer Beatty. He will interview you shortly." McDougall pointed to the officer who was already assembling the residents for questioning.

"You okay?" Sheriff McDougall asked of Franklin.

"Except for my hand, my chest, and my pride, I'm okay." Franklin lifted her mangled hand, gesturing toward her chest where Morton's door had smashed into her, knocking her over. "I knew better," she mumbled, shaking her head. "I knew better."

"Let me walk you over to the EMTs and get you checked out. You're from Buffalo View Village?"

Franklin nodded. "Yes. I'm here investigating a case."

"You won't be able to drive with that hand. They'll probably take you to the clinic here and get you fixed up. I'll take you to the station when they're done. We can talk then about what happened here."

"Yes. I will need to call my captain." Franklin reached for her phone, realizing it was in her car. "Grab my phone, would you?"

McDougall left her to retrieve the phone. As he walked away, June Franklin, for the first time in a long while, felt the stirring of an interest in a romantic sort of way. Ian McDougall was handsome, kind, and smelled so good, she couldn't shake the scent of him. For a moment, Franklin lifted out of her pain and allowed herself to feel like a woman who could still like a man.

"I'll make the call for you. You're not going to be able to do it yourself, right?"

June did not like the feeling of helplessness and the nearness of McDougall caused her to blush a little. She liked that even less. "Please."

McDougall introduced himself to her captain and explained what he knew of the situation as Franklin was examined by an EMT. "Yeah. Looks like the hand is broken up. She'll be at the Mission County Medical Clinic. I'd say, give a few hours and pick her up at there. Oh, and the car's front end will need repair."

McDougall listened as Franklin's captain responded. "Hey, by the way, we've got a suspect in custody. I don't know anything about why your detective is here, though. Not yet." McDougall heard the captain's reply while watching the EMT work on Franklin. "No. I don't know who it is. I've got an officer taking him to lockup."

McDougall clicked off. "Wait up!" He called out to the EMT who was loading Franklin into the ambulance. McDougall jumped in the back with Franklin who was lifted into euphoria, partly from pain killers, but mostly from desire for the sheriff who was looking at her in that way that men look at women they desire. June shut her eyes, filtering all of her senses into the smell of the man so near she could touch if only her shattered hand could move.

At the clinic, Franklin's hand was x-rayed revealing less damage than expected. Only two fingers were broken, but the muscles and bones were deeply bruised. "It'll be a month or more before this heals enough to be of much use. And you'll need PT." The attending doctor seemed disinterested in the injuries to Franklin's hand. Her attention was more caught up by the bruising to Franklin's abdomen. "Get a CT of this." A nurse took over from the doctor to wheel Franklin away. "And be careful of that hand. Let me know when the CT results are up."

Dr. Maisy Short left the examining room to update Sheriff McDougall. "Mac." She announced herself to him in the most familiar way. "Your officer will be out of commission for a while. She's getting a CT on her abdomen. I'll let you know what we find. Is she new to the department?"

"Thanks Maisy. No, she's not one of ours. She's a detective from Buffalo View Village. Take good care of her, will you? We don't want to get a bad rep from our neighbors!" He laughed and smiled and sat back in his chair to wait for the next report.

The doctor, lanky and stunning to look at, smiled back, in sharp contrast to her abrupt manner with Franklin and the nurse. "Are we still on for dinner?"

McDougall studied Short's angular features, her flashing brown eyes that had drawn him in the first moment they met, and her lips—soft and eager or pursed and tight, depending on her mood. She was the most striking woman he'd ever seen. And smart. She was smart, never clingy, and easy to be with when she felt like it. But she didn't always feel like being easy to get along with and he'd been less and less inclined to spend his time with her. "Yeah, not tonight. I don't know what's going on with this case, so better not make plans. Sorry."

"Not a problem." Dr. Short smiled and turned, then scowled. She looked back at McDougall. "Should I be worried?"

"About what?" But when he spoke, he turned his head away from her ever so slightly.

"Okay, then. I'll update you as soon as I can." Short walked away while Ian McDougall closed his eyes, shutting her out, and waited.

"You are lucky. I expected much worse." Dr. Short

explained Franklin's injuries. "Your right kidney is bruised, but not bleeding. It will heal on its own, but you'll have to be careful for a while." The doctor handed Franklin an information sheet. "Read this and call my nurse if you have questions. Take medical leave for at least six weeks. I'll get you a prescription for pain and I strongly urge you to use it as directed." Short did not once look Franklin in the eye. "Your body will heal faster if it's not fighting the pain." She examined Franklin's hand one more time before splinting the broken fingers, wrapping it, and asking the nurse to set her arm in a sling. "You'll need to follow up with your primary care physician in a week."

"Thank you, doctor." Franklin adjusted the sling, grateful that there was no damage done to her right arm or hand. "I will." But Short had already left the room. She thanked the nurse who wheeled her to the curb outside the clinic, where Sheriff McDougall was waiting to take her to the police station. McDougall held the passenger side door open for her. It was tricky getting into the car without knocking her hand against anything. She wasn't successful, but the pain medication kept her discomfort tolerable. She closed her eyes during the ride, feeling the strong afternoon sun hot on her face. The smell of McDougall overwhelmed everything else.

"We're not going to get much talking done, are we?" McDougall grinned.

"Mmmmm, no, ummm." Detective Franklin was out cold and did not know how she got from his car to her home and into her own bed.

The next morning, she was awake by seven and on the phone with her captain. "I know, I know. Come by later and take my report." Still in bed, Franklin briefly wondered at her uniform neatly folded and set on a nearby chair. "I know. I was stupid." She rolled her eyes to the ceiling. "Yes. I know! But listen, you need to know that I went there to talk to Morton's parents. I didn't know he was there, and I didn't know they were planning to run. You've got to find those two – yeah, the parents. They rammed my car, and Morton's on their way out. License, make, model, notes are in the file." She struggled to sit up, using her body and not her broken hand. "And Captain, I'd keep Lorde out of this. We'll talk when I see you but assign somebody else."

June removed her sling and with the utmost care, began to remove her pajamas, the one set of pajamas she kept because they'd been a gift from her mother. They'd never been worn before this. June slept in a t-shirt and knit shorts if she wore anything at all. She was most often too tired to bother with dressing for sleep. *Who found them? Who went through my drawers? Who dressed me? And who laid out a clean t-shirt and jogging pants for me?* Now naked, she covered her arm in a plastic bag but couldn't figure out how to secure it when she heard the doorbell ring. As she tried to get into the fresh clothing, she heard someone enter her house and call her name.

"Detective Franklin? Are you awake?" A woman's voice called out to her.

"I'm up here. Give me a minute." June wrapped a light blanket around her shoulders. "Who are you?"

"It's Gloria Stanche, Detective. I've come with my neighbor, Lucille, to help you this morning."

June sat on the bed, already worn out. "Okay. Come on up."

"Put those muffins in the kitchen, would you, Lucille, while I go upstairs to help Detective Franklin." Gloria made her way to Franklin's bedroom. "We've brought you some breakfast muffins. Do you have coffee in the mornings?" She found the detective half dressed with the plastic bag around her wrist. "Oh, let me help you with that." Gloria secured the plastic up to June's elbow, using duct tape that sat on June's dresser.

June watched Mrs. Stanche fuss over her. "Why are you here? I don't mean to be rude, but I don't understand why you're here."

"You don't remember?"

June shook her head.

"I was here last night to help you. The church was called to send someone to check on you and get whatever you needed. The reverend's wife, Lucille, called me to come with her. She's downstairs with the muffins. I helped you get undressed. Sheriff McDougall didn't seem to know what to do, so I sent him on his way."

McDougall. Oh God. "I'm fuzzy about how I got here. Thank you for being here then and today." June stood up to test her strength and balance. She'd seen enough strung-out people to know how pain meds affect judgment and mobility. "I think I'm good to get into the shower on my own. I'll let you know if I need something."

Gloria left the room but stayed near, listening for any sound of trouble.

The shampoo bottle slipped out of June's hand and landed on her foot when she tried to squeeze the liquid onto her head. "Ouch! Ouch! Dammit!"

"Are you all right?" Gloria was at the bathroom door in a flash.

"Yeah. Yeah. I dropped the shampoo on my foot. I'm okay." June managed the best she could to wash and rinse her hair, soap up and rinse off her body, then get out of the shower and towel off. She opened the bathroom door and was met with Gloria's arm, her head turned away, holding clean underwear, the fresh t-shirt, and pants.

"Thank you, Mrs. Stanche. You can go downstairs now."

June took the clothing and waited to dress until she was certain Mrs. Stanche was gone.

Dressed and towel-dried, June walked downstairs. Just before she reached the kitchen, she heard the two women chattering and a third voice, a male voice responding. She smelled his aftershave before she saw him. June peered into the kitchen where Ian McDougall was being served a muffin and coffee. He raised his eyes to her and winked.

"Good morning, detective. Glad to see you ready to go to work."

CHAPTER 12

Mrs. Person's Crush

Gloria turned to look at Detective Franklin. "Good Lord! You must sit down immediately!"

June held her abdomen as her face blanched, her eyes shut, and her legs began to buckle. Gloria and McDougall reached for her, Ian catching her from the back as June slumped into his arms. Gloria let go. "Please, can you get her back upstairs? I'll bring a pitcher of water and a glass. She needs to take a pill and sleep."

Ian guided her up the steps and into her bedroom. He sat her in the chair, straightened the sheets and blanket on the unmade bed. "Maybe we'll work tomorrow." He helped June to her feet, got her into bed, and straightened the bedding around her. "Or maybe not." He winked at her again. His fragrance was everywhere in her room. She sat up as best she could when Mrs. Stanche entered. With outstretched hand, Gloria helped June take the medication while the sheriff stood back. "I'll check in later. By the way," he spoke as he turned to leave the room, "we've got the Stanches in custody."

Gloria stopped still. "Who?"

June tried to caution McDougall, but instead, slid down in

her bed, unable to speak or gesture, and let the pain killer work its magic.

"Sheriff," Gloria stopped McDougall's exit. "I am Gloria Stanche. Who do you have in custody?"

McDougall stepped backwards into the room and turned on his heel to face Gloria. "You're who?"

~~~~

Lucille Persons sat at Detective Franklin's kitchen table with her head in her hands. She stared at the coffeemaker and listened to it beep as it shut itself off. The smell of brewed coffee mingled with the sugary sweet odor from the basket of apple spice muffins in front of her made her hungry and nauseous at the same time. Morning sunlight warmed the back of her head. She closed her eyes, imagining Gloria Stanche near her as she built up the courage to express her romantic feelings. The sounds of Gloria and the sheriff coming down the stairs prompted her to her feet.

"How is she?" Lucille didn't give them time to answer before asking if they wanted fresh, hot coffee.

Gloria ignored her question, patting the sheriff on his arm. "I think it's best if you leave her to rest for a few days, at least until she can see her own doctor. She doesn't look well. I don't know if you are aware of the extent of her injuries, but her entire abdomen is black with bruising."

Lucille raised an eyebrow. "How do you know that?"

Gloria again ignored Lucille. "It's not just her broken hand. She's seriously hurt. I don't know why she isn't in the hospital."

Sheriff McDougall nodded. "I know. The doc at our hospital filled me in." He looked at both of the women. "But she's a cop. We don't, as a general rule, like to quit working, no matter what. She needs to know that we need her. That will help her recover faster than any hospital stay." His hand on the kitchen doorknob, he said goodbye.

"Wait!" Lucille handed him some muffins wrapped up in a paper towel. "Take these with you."

"Thank you, Mrs. Persons." He turned back to face them again. "Are you here all day with her? Does she have anybody else?"

"She has the entire Buffalo View Village supporting her. She will be fine in our care." Gloria was certain she was reading Sheriff McDougall correctly as she suspected his romantic inclinations toward Detective Franklin. "And I understand her captain will be here later, so you can be assured that all her personal and professional bases are covered. Thank you for getting her here, sheriff." At that, McDougall was dismissed by Gloria, and he almost forgot that her last name was Stanche.

"Wait. I would like to speak with you before I go."

"Yes, I'd nearly forgotten. Let's go outside." Gloria left Lucille wondering what was going on between the sheriff and her friend. She walked the sheriff to his car. "Who do you have in custody? The Stanches?"

Sheriff McDougall promptly wrested the inquisition from Gloria and began his own. "Gloria Stanche. Is that a married name?"

Gloria nodded. "Yes, my husband died nine years ago under suspicious circumstances. Detective Franklin is trying to find out what happened to him and his body."

"Who is Morton Stanche to you?"

"He's nobody to me, except he showed up the other day and seems to be responsible for or part of a ploy to unnerve me. Detective Franklin will have to explain it all to you when she can." Gloria's face relaxed into exhaustion. "These last few days have been terrible and now this." She looked away from McDougall for a moment, then back again. "But who do you have in custody?"

"Do you know Walter and Lorinda Stanche?"

Gloria's full attention was back on the sheriff. "Who? Julian's parents, I think. Why?"

"I have to get going, Mrs. Stanche. I'll be in touch."

Sheriff McDougall got into his car and drove off leaving a bewildered Gloria Stanche in the driveway, by herself, feeling the now too familiar rise of anxiety and shock.

She stood in the driveway until Lucille called her back inside. "What are you doing out there?"

Gloria took a deep breath and turned to walk into the house. "Nothing. That sheriff said he has three people with the last name of Stanche in custody." She shook her head and her body as though she could rid herself of the ever-mounting pile of bad news. "Let's have some coffee and one of those muffins you brought along."

Lucille served her friend then sat down across from her at the table. "Are you all right? You've been through so much!"

Gloria, with a mouthful of muffin, nodded. She sipped her coffee, washing down the muffin morsels, and cleared her throat. "Honestly, Lucille. I have no idea. We have our poor Detective Franklin badly injured, and it appears that her injuries are my fault." Lucille attempted to object. "No, Lucille, it's because she was working on my case that this happened to her. I'm certain of it." Gloria ate another bite of muffin and chased it down with another sip of coffee. "But that McDougall is a handsome one, don't you think?"

Lucille stammered. "I … I suppose. I really wasn't paying any attention." She looked adoringly at Gloria. "I was worried about you and of course, Detective Franklin. How can I help? Is there anything I can do?"

Gloria shook her head. "I don't know. I really don't know. Anything." She finished her muffin and coffee. "I'm going to look in on our patient and then I'm going home if you will stay with her until her captain comes by."

"I will. Of course, I will. But, Gloria, what about you? Can I come by later and fix you some lunch or get you anything?"

Gloria took a long look at Lucille. Perhaps she'd misjudged her intentions. "You're being such a good friend, Lucille. I happily accept your invitation of lunch or an early dinner. That depends on the arrival of the captain."

Lucille beamed. "All right then. It's settled. I will check in on you as soon as I can."

Back at home, Gloria wasted not one moment to climb the stairs to her room, crawl into her bed, and fall into a deep, dreamless sleep. She was awakened, sometime later by Lucille gently tapping her arm. Gloria startled and sat straight up, causing The Cat to move barely a muscle. Though the room was bright, it seemed late in the day.

"What are you doing in here?" She snapped at Lucille.

"I'm sorry, but you've been sleeping so long, I thought you would want to get up. I've brought a green bean casserole and porkchops. They're warming in your oven."

Gloria slipped into her slippers, and with no apology to Lucille asked, "How long have I been sleeping?"

"It's been about four hours." Lucille stood back while Gloria walked to the stairway.

"Well, come on then." Both women proceeded down the stairs while The Cat raced to be first to the kitchen. "Let me feed the cat and then tell me about the detective." She realized how rude she was being and apologized. "I'm sorry I'm cranky. It's the long nap. The food smells like heaven! Would you like to join me?"

Lucille smiled and quickly agreed. "I'll set the table if you'll point me to the dishes and flatware." Once the table was set, she filled the plates. "Water, juice?"

"There is some lemon water in the refrigerator."

"Perfect!" Lucille filled the glasses then sat down across from Gloria. "I'm sorry about all that's happened to you." She spoke while arranging a paper napkin on her lap. "Thank you for letting me be a help to you."

Gloria, a forkful of porkchop up to her mouth, replied. "I appreciate you and your willingness to help me," and then she smiled at Lucille. "And I especially appreciate this meal!"

Lucille's face flushed, unnoticed by Gloria as she devoured her food. The women ate in silence until the last bit of beans and chops were consumed. Lucille stood to clear the table, but Gloria stopped her.

"No, not yet. Tell me about the detective and how she's doing. Did she get some rest before her captain showed up?"

Yes, actually. And her doctor arrived at the same time and gave her a good going over. He wouldn't tell me anything but after they left, Detective Franklin told me she'd be up on her feet in about three weeks."

"That sounds much better than what I imagined! Thank the Lord!"

"We don't need to stay with her any longer. The clinic sent over a helper to keep an eye on her and make sure she's eating and taking her meds as she should. She seems to be accepting of the care and willing to follow the rules." Lucille finished giving her status report.

"Well, then. Let's clean up here and sit out in the garden for a while. Do you have time for that?"

Lucille's heart skipped a beat. "I do!" She was on her feet in a flash.

Gloria and Lucille sat together on the bench by the bubbling fountain in the garden. It was only five o'clock, but the air had the feeling of rain or cooling coming soon. The Cat dashed under a large hosta and settled in, peering out from beneath its leaves, watchful for prey that may pass by.

They were quiet for some time. Lucille reveled in the nearness of Gloria. She dared not disturb the space that held them together. Like the cat, she was watchful for an opportunity, but kept still, hoping Gloria could not hear the pounding of her heart.

"What a lovely evening." Gloria sighed. "I wish I could roll back the last couple of days and make them disappear from history." Lucille remained silent, allowing Gloria to confide her feelings without interruption. Gloria looked at Lucille. "Do you think my husband will ever be found?"

Lucille was startled. "I don't know anything about him, except for neighbor chatter. He's been gone, nine years is it?"

Gloria nodded. "Yes. His body has not been discovered. Although now that the police have those hand bones, maybe that will tell us something." Gloria's shoulders drooped a little. "It's all so frightening. Even with the people in custody – well, I don't know why, and I don't know who they are, and I don't know what they have to do with me or Julian."

Gloria watched as The Cat stretched out a paw, then the other, raising its body to stalking posture. "I feel a bit like that bird over there."

Lucille turned to see The Cat about to pounce on an oblivious fox sparrow. She moved closer to Gloria and reached out for her hand. "You are quite afraid, aren't you?"

"I am." The sparrow was up and away before The Cat could reach it. "I feel like I'm being watched like that, but I don't have the instinct to flee in time."

"That settles it, Gloria. I'm going to collect some things and come to stay with you until you have answers and feel safe."

Gloria did not object and remained seated in the garden until Lucille returned and settled into her house.

CHAPTER 13

Roland Blue Fox

Gloria woke up to bright sunlight in her room, the noisy sounds of lawn mowers, and neighbor's chatting as they walked past her house. The Cat was gone. Gloria glanced at the clock on her bedside table as she bent to pull on her slippers. "Ten-thirty!" She shouted the words out loud.

Lucille called upstairs to her. "You're awake? If you're ready to come downstairs, I'll make some breakfast. How about eggs? How do you like your eggs?"

Gloria did not answer, but dressed, made her bed, and left the room.

"Good morning!" Lucille was far too chipper for Gloria's taste.

"Good morning, Lucille. I don't need any breakfast. But yes, one of your muffins and some coffee will do." Gloria sat at the table struggling not to glare at Lucille. "I appreciate that you stayed last night. I was tired, done in. But I'm okay now."

"You need a few days to get fully rested." Lucille's face

was flushed and her speech a touch manic.

"We'll see. You need to understand that I am used to living alone. As much as I appreciate the help this morning, allowing me to sleep in, this is not at all normal for me. I need to get back to my routine." But exhaustion showed in her face. "Where is my cat?"

"I fed him earlier and he's been outside since then." Lucille sat down next to Gloria. "Look, I know you want things to be normal, but they're not. These last few days have been extraordinary and cruel. With people in custody and so many questions unanswered, I urge you to take a few days to catch your breath and balance. Honestly, Gloria, it's too much for anyone."

Just then there was a knock at the kitchen door. Lucille and Gloria stood in unison, but Gloria gestured to Lucille to stay put. Ruth Claresman was leaving a package just as Gloria opened the door. "More seeds?"

Ruth shook her head. "Good morning, Mrs. Stanche. I don't know what's in here." She lifted the package and handed it to Gloria.

"Yes, more seeds. Can you stop in for a cup of coffee or don't they allow that?"

Ruth shook her head again. "I'm sorry. I'd like to. But no, I can't. Mostly because I'm trying to get done early today. I'm going to be looking at bridal bouquets." Her cheeks flushed as she smiled. "But I've heard that you are the one to ask about that."

"I would love to talk to you about your flowers. Can you come back around, say four o'clock? We'll talk in the garden."

"Thank you. But I forgot to ask, how are you?"

"I'm fine. And I want to thank you for helping me. I do feel much better, and I have plenty of police working on my behalf. I don't expect any further upset here. Please come by this afternoon and we'll talk about your wedding plans and beautiful flowers."

"Thank you, Mrs. Stanche. Thank you so much. I'll be back

later."

The Cat appeared and rubbed against Gloria's leg. "Good kitty," she said as she reached for him. At that moment, the three boys who had taunted Gloria walked by. They jeered at her and took off running down the street. The Cat slipped through the cat door leaving Gloria emptyhanded. She began to cry.

"Oh, Gloria," Lucille was watching her beloved from the kitchen window and raced to her side. "Come in. Come in. Sit. Rest. I'm here. You don't need to do anything. I'm here."

She wrapped her arm around Gloria's shoulder, longing to pull the woman closer, even to kiss her. But Gloria straightened herself up, pushed Lucille's arm away, wiped her tears, and entered the house on her own strength.

"Lucille, please, don't hover. Please, just stop. I don't want to be rude, but I really think you should go. I'm not sick. I'm not an invalid. I just need to rest."

Lucille hoped for more time with Gloria, time to reveal her heart. "I'll pack my things after I clean up the kitchen."

"Thank you for understanding." Gloria, with The Cat in her arms, returned to her bedroom.

Lucille put the few dishes in the dishwasher, wiped down the counter and table and resolved to make herself as available as need be. It was clear that Gloria needed someone now and she was determined to be the one Gloria would lean on.

~~~~

At four o'clock, Ruth Claresman with her fiancé, Micky Blue Fox, arrived in Gloria's backyard. A table was placed near the fountain, set with rose-patterned plates and cups, and a stack of florist's trade magazines Gloria saved over the years.

Ruth and Mickey walked hand-in-hand through Gloria's

gardens, pointing at the beautiful blossoms and stopping to inhale the sweetness of the yellow tea roses. Gloria, on her way from the house with a tray of iced coffee and glazed raspberry scones, stood still to watch the couple move as one. She sniffled a little, fighting back tears of joy or sadness—she didn't know which emotion brought the tears, maybe both. Gloria was deeply moved by their affection and pleasure in each other.

"Ruth, Mickey, come join me." She set the tray on the table and took the seat nearest the fountain.

"We appreciate your time, Mrs. Stanche." Ruth and Mickey sat, shoulder to shoulder. "Your gardens are spectacular." Ruth held her cup as Gloria poured iced coffee, then placed a scone on her plate.

"I'm happy you think so. My gardens are my passion." She filled Mickey's cup and set a scone on his plate. "Mickey, I don't believe I've seen you since you went off to college. I hear you're going to law school in the fall."

"That's the plan, Mrs. Stanche, after I marry this treasure." Mickey lifted Ruth's hand to kiss, just as a bee landed on her pollen-covered fingers. "Ouch! He got me in the lip!"

Ruth examined the bee sting with her forefinger. "You're not allergic, are you?"

"No. Only embarrassed!" He tried to smile as his lip swelled, but not enough to cause concern.

"I'll get you an ice pack for that." Gloria left the couple to consider Mickey's wound while she retrieved the ice pack and calamine lotion.

"We love the bees," she said as she handed Ruth the ice pack, "but sometimes they mistake us for an enemy!"

"Speaking of enemies," Mickey's speech was altered slightly because of his swollen lip. "Ruth told me you've had some trouble lately—serious trouble. Is it anything my dad can help you with?"

"Oh, Mickey, that's kind of you. I actually hadn't considered legal representation. I'm not sure why I would need his help. On the other hand, maybe I do. I'll call him later to get his thoughts." Gloria sat down and looked off into the gardens. The Cat was stretched out on hot stone pavers, soaking up the heat from them and the sun as well. She wondered that he didn't roast a little.

"But you're here to talk about flowers for the bouquet. What about for the church, and the groomsmen, and the mothers. You can't forget the mothers! And the reception hall!"

For three hours, they visited and poured through magazines, at last settling on a color scheme and floral arrangements. Gloria volunteered to create a list of sources and prices to make the ordering process easy for the couple. "If there is any other way I can help you with your plans, please ask. I would want to help anyway, but especially because of your care and consideration of me, Ruth, in these last few days."

Ruth and Mickey gathered up the magazines and said goodbye. Gloria called for The Cat as she collected plates and cups and headed back toward the house. It was a warm evening that fell on her like a shawl covering shivering shoulders. She felt the now too-familiar feeling of anxiety build.

"Let's get you some dinner," she spoke to The Cat as he trotted, tail up, beside her. They entered the house, side-by-side. Gloria tried to shake the feeling of dread but could not. "Early to bed, I think, for both of us."

After filling the cat bowl, she fixed a plate of leftovers from the foods brought by Lucille, then sat at the kitchen table, staring out the window. She must have fallen asleep sitting up in her chair, food untouched, when she startled and jumped at the sound of someone knocking on the front door. The Cat was long gone. The clock read 9:30. The house was dark. Gloria turned on lights as she passed from the kitchen through to the living room, then flipped on the outside light at the front door.

"Hello, Mrs. Stanche. I thought I'd stop by to catch up. My son tells me you've had some troubles. I wonder if I might help."

Gloria opened the door to see Roland, the father of Mickey Blue Fox. He looked the same as always, barely aged, even in his mid-fifties. His beautiful thick black hair, his eyes the color of chocolate, his warm, disarming smile reminded her that she'd had a crush on him in her sophomore year. *We were just children*, she thought as she realized she was staring. "Please, please come in Roland."

"You can call me Ron, Gloria." Roland looked around. "May I sit over there?"

Gloria nodded. "Anywhere, Ronal ... Ron." He sat in her reading chair while she settled herself on the sofa.

Just then, The Cat appeared and jumped onto Roland's lap. He stroked The Cat and talked softly to it while commenting to Gloria on what a nice cat she had. Gloria was stunned. The Cat didn't warm up to anyone else, ever.

"Roland," Gloria felt uncomfortable referring to him as Ron. "You could have called?" Her tone suggested a question. "I must say, I'm awfully tired this evening. Could we do this another time?"

"We certainly can," Roland replied as he set The Cat on its feet on the carpet. "I want you to know that I am available to you the minute you need legal counsel. I will clear my calendar to suit you, if at all possible."

"Why would you do that for me? Honestly, we haven't seen each other in so many years."

"I understand that the police have Morton Stanche in custody, looking for enough evidence to hold him for further charges. I believe I have what they need, but I'd like to consult with you first."

"How on earth do you know anything about Morton Stanche?" Gloria was shocked.

"That's what I'd like to talk with you about. But I can see you are extremely tired. We can do this another time." Roland brushed the cat hair from his pants and stood to leave. "Here's my card. Call me as soon as you're up to it." He handed Gloria his business card. "I urge you to talk to me before talking further to the police."

Gloria remained sitting as Roland Blue Fox let himself out. The Cat mewed and stared at her. *What now*, she wondered. She hushed The Cat, scooped him up in her arms, locked the front door, turned off the downstairs lights, and headed up the stairs.

Just then she heard a knock at the door. This time it was the kitchen door. She peered around the corner of the staircase to see a shadowy figure poised to knock again. "Go away!" she shouted. "Go away!"

"Mrs. Stanche, Gloria, it's me, Charlie Boone. We need to talk."

Gloria, now at the kitchen door, raised her voice. "No, Mr. Boone, we do not. Not now."

He began pounding on the door. "But we do. Blue Fox was just here, was he not? You need to listen to me before you say anything else to him!"

"You need to go now, or I will call the police. This is stalking! A crime! Go!" Gloria was angry and shaking. The Cat leapt from her arms to the floor, rubbing his body against her legs as if to provide soothing comfort. She searched her pockets for the phone. The Cat jumped onto the kitchen table and began licking Gloria's cold, untouched meal.

"Get down!" The Cat did not get down but walked across

her phone, then sat down to lick its paws. She could hear Boone's car leaving her driveway.

Gloria collected the phone and dishes from the table. She scraped the plate clean, emptied her water glass, put the dishes in the dishwasher and took out the garbage, letting The Cat out for one last venture outdoors. She settled herself on the garden bench and closed her eyes, inhaling the evening's garden fragrance. Calmed, she opened her eyes, retrieved her phone, and called Detective Franklin.

CHAPTER 14
Sheriff McDougall

The Detective did not answer. The phone rang countless times before dropping Gloria into voicemail. "Detective Franklin, this is Gloria Stanche. I hate to disturb your rest, but if you would text me the name and number of who I should talk to about my case, then I won't be calling you again until you're back on your feet." Gloria paused. "And if you need anything, please let me know. Thank you."

She called for The Cat who was already at her side. Together they walked up the stairs and settled into bed for a much-needed night of uninterrupted sleep.

Sleep rolled in, knocking Gloria clear of the day's miseries. She dreamed of Roland Blue Fox, dancing with her at their junior prom. He brushed her hair with kisses. He took her hand to walk her off the dance floor. Gloria's heart pounded with excitement. Would he kiss her full on the lips? Would he ask her to be his girlfriend? What would her mother say? He touched her face lightly. She woke up to The Cat pawing her cheek. It was already past eight o'clock in the morning.

Gloria did not remember sleeping at all, though the feeling

of Roland's kisses was real enough. She rolled over on her stomach and groaned. *I can't start another day with turmoil.* But of course, this was a different type of disturbance from the previous days' terrors. Gloria was long overdue for romance. Even with the reopened wounds to her heart around Julian, she realized there was room for another. Even with her questions about Roland's cryptic and mysterious admonishment to talk to him first before anyone else, the dream of him stirred the truth that Gloria wanted a new romantic chapter in her life. She groaned again, rolled on her back, then sat up to get dressed, certain she was rested enough to face the new day.

Although it was past eight o'clock, the sun was not bright. She heard thunder slapping in the distance. Rain. Rain. "Oh, Lord!" She jumped out of bed, still in her nightclothes, shut the bedroom window as the wind picked up and the sky darkened. She dressed in the gloomy room, made her bed, and headed down to the kitchen. "Come on kitty," she called to The Cat who was already four steps ahead of her.

It was pouring outside when she turned on the kitchen light. She opened the door to the screened porch and inhaled the sweet smell of earth in a rainstorm. With the windows closed, she watched the rain pelt pavers and plants. *Beautiful rain*, she thought. *Quiet.* The Cat stuck its nose out of the cat door and pulled back in a flash. He jumped onto the porch bench and curled up against a pillow. Gloria walked into the house to get a cup of coffee and make herself some toast. Boone appeared yet again and began pounding at her door.

She didn't look at the man but shouted. "Go away!"

He continued pounding. "We have to talk!"

"No, we don't and if you don't leave me alone, I will call the police—again—to report you as a stalker!"

"Gloria, please."

"Go." She reached for her phone with no intention of dialing. "Now."

Boone got in his car but did not drive away.

Gloria took her coffee into the living room, sat in her reading chair, and did not open the drapes. *Does Boone have anything to do with Roland?* she wondered. The phone out of her pocket, her finger about to begin punching in Roland's number from his card, she stopped herself to think this through. *I'll wait to hear from Detective Franklin. Meanwhile, I will clean every bit of dirt out of this house.* By three o'clock, the house was cleaned from upstairs to downstairs, all the laundry was washed and put away, a chicken cacciatore casserole baked in the oven, and not a single soul had interrupted her. Which gave her hours to think and rethink what she wanted to do about Roland Blue Fox.

Gloria opened up the kitchen windows, noting that the rain stopped, the sun was shining, and Boone's car was gone. She pulled back the drapes in the living room, opened a book, and sat down to read for the remainder of the afternoon. Around 5:30 p.m., The Cat strolled in with a meow, asking for its supper, waking Gloria who had fallen asleep and slept straight through the dinging of the timer on her oven. The stench of burned casserole and rancid smoke, heavy in the air, got her to her feet. She raced to the kitchen, pulled out the burnt food and ran the casserole outside to cool off on the garden bench. Back in the smelly, smoky house, she set fans in place to clear the air, then filled The Cat's bowl and set it on the porch. He was nowhere to be found. She called and called but The Cat didn't come. He was busy feasting outside on overcooked chicken and potatoes.

By the time Gloria went to bed, she could count only one catastrophe for that day, and it was a catastrophe of her own making. *Tomorrow I'll ask Lucille back for a few days.* Gloria accepted the truth that she was simply too tired to get by without help.

~~~~

Ian McDougall was sitting on a chair next to Detective Franklin. He'd been sitting there for a while, waiting for Franklin to wake up. Her captain asked him to work the case with her, she'd agreed, and he arrived at her house for their first scheduled meeting. The neighbor, Lucille Persons, was back for another caregiver shift. She let McDougall in and left to go about her personal business as he agreed to keep an eye on the detective until she returned.

McDougall was a man cognizant of detail. He took note of the particulars in Franklin's room, the lack of a feminine style – no lace or frills or soft colors. There was no evidence of makeup or perfumes, but those items might be placed in the bathroom or a cupboard. The only items that revealed anything of Franklin's personality were the stack of books by her bedside and on her plain, highly polished, honey oak-stained dresser. No popular fiction. These were books you read to learn from, not to be entertained.

Another hour passed. Mrs. Persons returned with groceries. She was making lunch for Gloria when the sheriff came downstairs. "I'd nearly forgotten you were here. Would you like something to eat?"

"I would, thank you. I can't stay much longer. Will you be waking her up?"

"Yes. She needs to take some medication on a full stomach. I have vegetable soup and I can make a sandwich." Lucille was already pulling bread from its bag. "Is egg salad okay?"

"Sure, thanks."

Lucille handed him a sandwich and made a tray of soup

and a glass of water for him to carry upstairs to Detective Franklin. "I'll be right behind you with her pill."

"Franklin. Franklin." McDougall's voice was soft as he encouraged the detective to wake up. "I've got your lunch."

Franklin stirred, opened an eye, and closed it again. She mumbled something about giving her a minute to wake up. She tried to sit up as Lucille entered the room.

"Oh, let me help you!" Lucille set the pill on the lunch tray, shoving McDougall out of her way. With her arm around Franklin, she gently raised the woman's body forward, sliding pillows at her back to help support her. Franklin, more alert now, straightened herself and her bedding so she could sit upright and be comfortable. Lucille reached for the pill on the lunch tray.

"Here, take this. You're overdue." Lucille handed the pill to Franklin who took it with a gulp of water.

"How long was I asleep?"

"Close to six hours! You should probably try to move about a little. Can I help you to the bathroom?"

Franklin glanced at McDougall. "Would you mind?"

"Sorry." He put the tray on her dresser and left the room.

Once Franklin was situated in her bed again, she thanked Lucille, who handed her the lunch tray. "Would you ask the sheriff to come in now?" Lucille nodded as Franklin reached for her phone. "Oh, let me get that." With phone in hand, Franklin began to check calls. "Stop! Detective, you need to eat something first or the pill will make you sick!"

Franklin complied, eating half the sandwich before looking at her phone again. She scanned the messages, noting the call from Gloria Stanche the evening before. She listened to the message just as McDougall re-entered the room.

"Have you talked to the captain yet? I don't know that our counties are working together on this case."

"Yeah. We talked yesterday but it doesn't sound like he knows much. You haven't made a report yet, right?"

"Obviously not. We talked too, but I was pretty out of it. I'm still out of it." Detective Franklin could feel exhaustion sweeping through her body again. "Can we try tomorrow, maybe around nine? Let Mrs. Persons know when you all are coming here so she can help me get ready."

"I'll call him and let you know if he can work it out." McDougall ate the rest of his sandwich then cleared his throat. "Listen, I'm sorry you got beat up like this."

"Yeah, me too."

"Tomorrow?"

"Yes." Detective Franklin watched the sheriff leave her room. The scent of his aftershave lingered. She inhaled and smiled, snuggling into her sheets.

Lucille arrived to retrieve the lunch tray and ask Franklin if she needed anything else. "Ginger and Stella will take shifts for the rest of the day. I'm not sure who will be here overnight. I'm staying with Gloria Stanche in the evenings until she recovers from the stress of the last few days."

"Thank you all for everything you're doing for me." Franklin looked at her phone. "I should make some calls before I fall asleep again." But she was already nodding off.

Lucille smiled as she picked up the tray and turned to leave. "Don't try to do too much. The doctor was clear about bed rest for two days. He'll be back then to examine you again. Oh, and we are all pleased to help you. We wish this hadn't happened, though."

After Lucille left her room, Franklin forced herself to return Gloria's call. "Mrs. Stanch, this is Detective Franklin returning your call. I can't help you until possibly tomorrow afternoon. I think you've met Sheriff McDougall. Maybe you could talk to him, or my captain. I don't know who has been assigned to cover me for now."

Gloria was listening to Franklin's message when the doorbell sounded at her front door. Sheriff McDougall was standing on the step. "You're timing is quite good. Detective Franklin just left me a message to talk to you while she is on the mend. Come in."

She gestured for the sheriff to remove his shoes and guided him into the living room. She did not offer food or drink. She was too tired to play hostess. "I know you are not on our police force. How much help can you be on my case?"

McDougall nodded. "Right. Well, I don't know at this point. But whatever we talk about will go in a report to your police captain. And I'll make sure Detective Franklin is kept in the loop. I don't think she'll be down for long."

"Thank you for that. She is the most competent of the officers I've had the displeasure to encounter since the upheaval began in my life. But now I have a new dilemma and I don't know who I can trust. I trust her. By default, I suppose, I will have to trust you."

Gloria sat forward in her easy chair. "Do you know Roland Blue Fox?" She did not wait for McDougall to answer. "He told me not to speak to anyone but him about my case. He said he knows things and we should meet. I only know him from high school, so I have no reason to trust or distrust what he says. But I don't know what he's referring to. He came to see me last night, uninvited, and after he left, Mr. Boone appeared, warning me off of Roland. So, Boone is apparently watching me and my house." Gloria rattled off her concerns without taking a breath.

"Mrs. Stanche, you should know that I'm not up to speed on your case, so I don't know what you're talking about. I came to tell you that we couldn't hold Morton's parents, but he's been charged with assaulting a police officer and is in jail for now."

Gloria interrupted. "I thought Julian's parents were dead. They are the same people, right?"

CHAPTER 15
Buffalo View Village Picnic Preparations

Sheriff McDougall sat back in his seat, preparing for a longer interview than he'd planned. "Why would you think they were dead?"

"Julian said they were. He said they died from the flu I think, after he graduated from high school." She stopped to think. "But he probably lied about that. Is that what you're telling me?"

"I'm telling you that we had them in custody but had to release them for lack of evidence of any crime. Walter Stanche is a dead ringer for Morton, but that doesn't mean he's the father. He could be an identical twin himself. I don't know what to tell you, but we'll look into this further."

Gloria told the sheriff everything she knew about Roland Blue Fox, everything but the dream that bothered her throughout the day. *It's like that with nightmares, too,* she thought. *Nightmares leave a residue of discomfort, just like this.* "You know..." Gloria hesitated before speaking further.

"Know what, Mrs. Stanche?"

Gloria shook her head. "It's nothing. I ..."

"It could be something. In my experience, a little

something can turn into a big something. Is it something you would mention to Detective Franklin?"

Gloria snapped to attention. "Why would I tell her and not you?" But she knew the answer to that question. Gloria was embarrassed.

"I don't think this is worth mentioning, but Roland's visit last night, odd enough in its own right, bothered me, even into my dreams. It's bothered me all day long." Gloria hesitated again. "I dreamed about Roland at our high school junior prom—that he was my date. But in fact, the prom was my first day with Julian. I was filled with anticipation about what might be for the two of us." Gloria shifted in her chair. "I know dreams do funny things, mix things around, but this seemed like something else. I can't put my finger on it."

"Mrs. Stanche, thank you for telling me this. There might be something to learn from it. Time will tell." The sheriff got to his feet. "I want to thank you for meeting with me. I'll be in touch if I have anything to share about the Stanches. Morton remains in custody, so you don't have to worry about him for the time being."

"Sheriff." Gloria remained seated, her face tight, expressionless. "Sheriff, I think Julian and Roland were lovers."

~~~~

The next few weeks passed by without further excitement. Morton Stanche was charged with assaulting an officer and remained in custody awaiting trial. The elder Stanches, as far as Gloria was aware, skedaddled straight out of the county straight from their respective jail cells. Detective Franklin was back on her feet and at work part time. She called Gloria to tell her that she was still investigating the incidents in Gloria's home and garden and hoped Gloria was doing well.

Gloria was doing better than that. She was engaged with planning and was enthusiastic and busy from daybreak to sunset, preparing for the Buffalo View Village Picnic. She crossed off her daily to-dos as the days flew by. With only three weeks before the village picnic plus Ruth and Mickey's wedding, there was much to do.

As president of the Buffalo View Village Garden Club, she found the need to delegate. Lucille was eager to help, and surprisingly to Gloria, was more than a great cook. Lucille became second in command, managing all but the most important aspects of the garden club tasks for the yearly picnic.

Lucille spent a good part of each day with Gloria to her devoted husband's dismay.

"But I want you here, with me, my love," he'd say.

She felt bad for him, knowing how much he loved her. But though she loved him too, she no longer felt passion as she had in the beginning of their marriage. At that time, she hadn't known that she could feel a deeper, more abiding love, and certainly not for a woman. She was changed by Gloria.

"Please, Lucille my pet, come to bed." He would entreat her. But she made excuses every night and avoided his attentions.

"Maybe after the picnic. There is much to do, and I can't disappoint Mrs. Stanche." Lucille stayed awake until sleep overpowered her waking dreams of Gloria in her arms.

~~~

Hank Broden was charged with finishing up the paint project he'd started on Gloria's house. When that was complete, he set about building a bridal trellis and stage for Ruth and Mickey's wedding. The Cat stayed out of his way.

Gloria's bridal wreath bush recovered from the earlier

damage. She was able to salvage sprigs of blossoms to dry for later use in arrangements. Her gardens were in full bloom, given it was the second week in July. They overwhelmed her at times with beauty, fragrance, and insect activity. Ruby throated hummingbirds hovered above orange honeysuckle blossoms, while bees of every size and shape sounded a choir of tones from soprano to alto to bass as they filled summer squash blossoms and covered zinnias. Butterflies visited white and blue phlox and hollyhocks. Daisies, Rudbeckia, daylilies and nasturtium, leant color and depth to every flowering garden bed. The roses, in pinks, yellows, whites, and reds were glorious in display. Annual grasses, interspersed with liatris, heather, and hostas provided haven for The Cat as it cooled from summer's heat.

Garden club members were due for a tour in under an hour and Gloria was running behind. "Lucille, would you please set up the buffet table across from the forsythia? The table covering is on the porch, inside the bench. Give it a good shake and try to smooth out the fold marks."

Ginger Spalding and Herman Edison were the first to arrive. Herman brought a folding table and Ginger pulled on a garden cart containing five large pots of plants. "Where would you like us to set up?" Ginger startled Lucille who was draping the luncheon table.

"Oh," I didn't hear you until you were at my elbow!" Lucille was flustered, as though Ginger may have guessed that her thoughts were not on the table settings. "Follow me. We'll set you up over here so everyone can see the arrangements."

Herman unfolded the table and brushed its surface clean with a damp cloth, then signaled to Ginger to bring the cart closer. "Let me help you lift those." Herman was a stout and affable man who enjoyed any and all social gatherings. "The sooner we get this done, the sooner we can have at that strawberry pie!"

As he and Ginger arranged the potted plant display for inspection and approval by the other garden club members, Lucille finished setting up the luncheon table. Meanwhile the Barry sisters, Nancy and Francine, arrived with picnic table centerpieces and Paulette Jensen came with samples for signage. The other seven members, including Larry Grainger, strolled in with their picnic displays for committee approvals. Within an hour, all were seated, waiting for the eating and the meeting to begin.

Gloria gave the nod to the garden club members' plans with little input this year. She was too tired to do much but fuss over every detail of the wedding plans. She was satisfied to sip lemonade and eat her lunch while the members approved plans and set a schedule. The Cat watched for birds and insects from beneath the hostas. It was a lazy, uneventful afternoon.

Lucille offered to clean up after the meeting. "Thank you, Lucille. I feel like I'm asking too much of you, but I do appreciate all your help." With that said, Gloria, with The Cat at her ankle, entered the house and laid down for a nap.

She dreamed of Ruth and Mickey's wedding and all the things that could go wrong. She woke in a sweat. It was eighty degrees outside with sun beaming into her room. She'd forgotten to turn on the fan. In fact, she'd forgotten how she got into bed in the first place. Gloria looked at the clock on her bedside table. *4:30!* She'd been asleep for at least two hours! The Cat jumped on the bed from the window seat. *I know, it's time for supper.* Gloria shook her head, ran her fingers through her hair, stepped into her shoes, and headed downstairs to the kitchen.

There was no knock at either door. There was nothing but calm in the street. No children were fighting or crying or yelling or laughing. No cars rolled past her house. A soft breeze ruffled the kitchen curtains as the late afternoon light began to fade away. The only sound was of the cat crunching its kibble. It was a perfect end to a perfect day.

The phone rang. Gloria hesitated before answering. "Yes, Lucille?"

"I'm calling to check on you, to see if you need anything."

"Thank you, but I'm all right. I needed a nap, but I feel refreshed. I feel as if a page has turned, leaving trouble in the last chapter!" Gloria surprised herself with a chuckle. "You did a great job today. I think we will have the best event ever this year."

"I think so too." Lucille's voice was bubbly with pleasure. "Everyone enjoyed the lunch, especially your strawberry pie. I thought all the plans came together beautifully."

"There are a few wedding details left to tackle, but then, well, I think we're ready." Gloria walked The Cat to the porch and out the door. She inhaled the sweet early evening air. "Yes, Lucille, it will be the best picnic ever!"

Gloria sat on the cast iron bench near the bubbling fountain. She thought about Larry Grainger and was grateful that he had made no overtures to her today. She'd barely noticed him, and he seemed intent to stay out of her way. But her dream about Roland Blue Fox still disturbed her and not only because she realized what she'd known all along; that Julian was gay. The Cat jumped up on the bench and kneaded Gloria's thigh. She scratched its ears and mumbled aloud, "They robbed me of true love."

She stood, ready to have an early evening inspection of the garden plants, when she heard a car door slam in the street near her house. Larry Grainger entered the backyard, tipping his straw hat to Gloria.

"Good evening." His manner was leisurely, as if he'd been invited and had not intruded into her evening and yard. "I want to clear some things up with you."

Gloria, having regained her strength, was well resolved to move out ahead of her troubles. "Mr. Grainger, you can leave and take up your issues with Detective Franklin. I'm not having a conversation with you about your actions. It is the job of the police department to examine your reasons. Now go." Gloria picked up The Cat as though to use it as a weapon.

"You don't understand." Larry Grainger protested.

"I don't need to. I don't need to know a single thing from you." Gloria moved closer to Grainger. "If you want me to start screaming, I will."

Gloria was serious and stern. The Cat yowled and squirmed to be set free. She bent over to release him and noticed Grainger take a step forward. "Don't you dare!" She pulled her phone from her pants pocket and pressed the emergency button. "911 is called."

"That wasn't necessary!" Grainer turned to leave.

Gloria's neighbor, the one whose porch door frame was shattered by a stray bullet, watched the entire exchange. "Good for you, Stanche!"

She'd been unaware of him and scowled. "Good for nothing just left!"

But of course, 911 was dispatched and sirens approached her house.

"I'm taking cover this time!" The old neighbor laughed and went back inside his house.

The Cat was already through the cat door and Gloria rounded the house to assure the officers who had pulled up in front of her home, that there was nothing to worry about. Not this time.

"But please do report this to Detective Franklin. She'll want to know that Grainger was back. After what, I don't know."

CHAPTER 16
The Investigation

"This is Thomas Littlehorn, our village historian." Detective Franklin introduced Sheriff Ian McDougall in Littlehorn's office at the history center.

Thomas rose from a modern, leather desk chair positioned in front of an antique rolltop desk and offered his hand to McDougall.

"June has told me what she can about your involvement in this case." Littlehorn cleared his throat, adjusted his glasses, and sat down.

Franklin gestured to a wooden library chair across from her. "Why, thank you, June." He smirked. She kicked the leg on his chair.

"I first met Thomas …

"I was June's fourth grade math teacher." Littlehorn interrupted with a beaming smile, proving his pride in the former student.

"Yes, but as the village historian he can prove a relationship between Bethany Lee Shifton—Mrs. Stanche's mother—Julian Stanche, and Morton Stanche. At first I thought that's what it was." She paused to retrieve a document from a file folder on her lap. "But I don't know now that Julian Stanche is party to this deal." She handed the document to McDougall. "Page 14. You see, there," Franklin pointed her finger at the margin of the document, "the handwritten initials in the margin, *M S*." McDougall nodded. "I thought they were meant to alert Morton to something in the document, but now I think he may have been a partner in the scheme and maybe, just maybe, Julian Stanche wasn't involved at all." She reached for her glass of water. "And I think *that* because of a conversation I had with Roland Blue Fox."

"Yeah. What's the story with that guy?" McDougall leaned forward with interest. "I met with Mrs. Stanche and she said he was at her house, warning her off of talking to anybody else. Not specific though. Just don't-say-a-word kinda deal."

"She called me. I told her that it was okay to talk to you, but to let me know what you talked about so we're all on the same page." Franklin took a drink of water and in the pause, Littlehorn jumped in.

"He's my cousin, you know, Roland. He's a good lawyer. He's gay, too. I don't think his kid knows that."

"Relevance?" Franklin bristled.

McDougall jumped in. "There is something. Mrs. Stanche brought it up."

"What?"

"Yeah. She said she had a dream about him, and it made her think that Blue Fox and her husband, Julian, might have been lovers in high school."

"Well then why," Franklin stammered, "why did Julian marry her?"

"Why do you think?" Littlehorn did not try to hide his disapproval.

"Gloria Stanche talks only of her love for him. Is that real or a show for us?" McDougall cast a quizzical eye at Franklin.

"How would I know?" She kicked McDougall's chair leg again.

"Listen you two, Littlehorn commanded. "Stop with the flirting! We've got important business here. I believe there's a plot of some sort to harm Gloria Stanche. I just can't put the pieces together."

Franklin and McDougall objected in unison. "We're not flirting!"

Littlehorn stared them down as if they were children in his classroom. "I don't know who you think you're fooling, but it's not me!" His voice softened. "Maybe you don't see what's in front of you. What kind of investigators does that make you? Do I need to be working this out with somebody else?"

Franklin apologized while McDougall continued to object. "I don't know what you're talking about. I've got a girlfriend." He looked at Franklin and sighed. "Well, okay. I had a girlfriend." He rolled his chair in closer to the others. "Let's get back to it, then."

~~~~~

Gloria accompanied Ruth for her final wedding dress fitting. "I'm so grateful that you can help me with all of this," Ruth, with a tear in her eye, smiled at Gloria. "My mom can't be here, nor my dad, or my sister. They don't like me marrying outside of the faith. That's how they put it."

"You can't please most of the people most of the time, Ruth. Are you happy?"

"I am. I am over the moon happy." Ruth entered the dressing room with the sales associate.

"I know Mickey is a good man and that's all I need to know. I'm delighted that you've included me in your plans. I don't have a daughter and didn't think I'd ever experience this." Gloria looked as relaxed as she ever had. "Plus, I get champagne while you dress!"

It wasn't long before Ruth stepped out from the dressing room to stand in front of a three-way mirror in the first gown. She and Gloria both shook their heads at the same time.

"Too much, right?" Ruth looked at Gloria for confirmation.

"Absolutely. Way too much. I'm always a fan of the understated. You are the bride wearing the dress, not the other way around."

The sales associate cocked an eye as if to hush Gloria from critique.

Gloria fired back, addressing Ruth while glaring at the associate. "Would you like me to help find the dress?"

Ruth and Gloria took their time combing through fabrics and laces and sequins and crystals. It took most of an hour for them to select five dresses. The associate took the dresses back into the dressing room so Ruth could try them on while Gloria had her second glass of champagne.

"That's the one!" Gloria nearly shouted when she saw Ruth in the third dress. That's it!"

Ruth agreed and the search began for a headpiece. Gloria suggested flowers instead. "Why spend all that money to cover your beautiful face? Such an old-fashioned bit of nonsense, right?"

Ruth laughed. "Mickey doesn't even care about the wedding day. He wants the party with his friends. So, flowers it is. You'll create it, right?"

Gloria took Ruth's hand and smiled. "Why do you think I suggested it?"

Gloria indulged in one more glass of champagne while Ruth changed into her street clothes and arranged to purchase the gown. Ruth would drive her home in plenty of time to clear her head, feed The Cat, and start dinner. All was right in Gloria's world that afternoon. She was oblivious to the red Jeep Wrangler Sport parked across the street from the bridal shop.

~~~~~

"So, here's what we have." Littlehorn dragged an ancient chalkboard on wheels over to the library table. He wrote all the pertinent names on the board while Franklin and McDougall called out whatever germane details they had about each one.

Morton Stanche. In custody for assaulting a police officer and resisting arrest.

"You know, the resisting arrest won't stick because I had no cause to arrest him."

"But he was fleeing the scene. Question is, what were you seeing that created an opportunity to cuff that family." McDougall was quick to chime in. "We still don't know why they were running – if that's what they were doing."

Franklin chimed in. "That takes us to Walter and Lorinda Stanche. I've got the photo of twin boys that don't like either of them. For that matter, we don't know if they're the parents or other relatives of Morton and Julian. And we don't know why Morton lied about his mother or if he did lie."

"Then there's that Charlie Boone guy." McDougall recounted what he knew which wasn't much. "It's pure chance that he was around to drive Mrs. Stanche home from the hospital. I gotta wonder, though, if he was such a close friend of her mother's, why didn't he introduce himself before? He's insisting that he is protecting her. All of a sudden? From what? Does he know more than he's letting on? Stanche thinks so."

"But she thinks everyone is plotting against her." Franklin sat forward in her chair. "I'm afraid she might be right."

"What's the deal with Grainger, the farmer. He's professing his love for Stanche while sneaking around inside her house. What's he up to?" McDougall shifted in his chair, causing it to roll backward on the uneven flooring.

"I haven't been out there to talk to him." Franklin made a note in her phone to visit Grainger at his farm.

Littlehorn wrote Bethany Lee Shifton on the board. "We know she was in a bogus land deal, maybe with Julian, more likely with Morton. But we don't know anything except that $750,000 is unaccounted for. But we don't even know what account." Littlehorn scribbled the word, money, on the board. "Isn't this the engine for every crime?'

McDougall nodded. "It's up there with jealousy and revenge."

"Mrs. Stanche believed her husband was cheating on her with other women, but it looks as if it was men, or a man instead. Who? And would that man or men have anything to do with his disappearance? How would that involve money? It has to be about money, right, because the others would only care if they gained from Julian's disappearance or death." McDougall rolled his chair back up to the library table. "It has to be about money. But why now? He's been out of the picture for nine years."

"Who did we leave out?" Littlehorn was poised to write more names.

"There's your cousin, Roland Blue Fox. He claims to know something about all of this." Franklin made another note in her phone. "I'll meet with him, too."

"The only people left are Gloria and Julian Stanche. I promised her that I would make his disappearance my priority. Anybody think he's alive?"

The room was silent. "Me either. We need to find his body. But to do that, we need to find who killed him. It could be any one of these people, well, except for Gloria."

They all agreed that Mrs. Stanche was being terrorized for a reason. "Money. It's got to be the money. But what money? Whose money?"

"Let's break for lunch." Littlehorn was getting frustrated. "Maybe if we walk away from this for a little bit, we'll come back with fresh minds."

~~~~~~

Ruth and Gloria left the bridal shop and got into Ruth's car. "Oh, I've left my purse and keys in the shop. I'll be right back." Ruth left the car to get her keys as Gloria settled into the passenger seat, feeling the glow and tingle of champagne run through her body. She barely noticed when the passenger side door was yanked open. A man who looked exactly like Julian, but much older than he would be, stared her in the eye.

"Do you want to see Julian? I know where he is."

The sound of his voice was so like Julian's, he looked so much like Julian, she believed that he did know where her husband was, dead or alive. Champagne perhaps interfered with Gloria's judgment, but sobriety would not have changed her response in the moment. She nodded to the man and stepped out from Ruth's car. He took her by the arm as if to help her, then pulled her in close to his side.

"I have a loaded pistol and I'm willing to use it, so keep your mouth shut and come with me."

~~~~~~

Detective Franklin felt her phone vibrate in her hand. "Hello? What? … When? … Where? … I'm on my way!" She clicked off the phone. "McDougall, come with me. Gloria Stanche is missing." Littlehorn rose from his chair. "No," Franklin said, "I can't have anyone know you're working with us on this." Littlehorn nodded and watch as Franklin and McDougall raced out the door.

At the bridal shop, there were already three squads surrounding Ruth Clarendon's car. Ruth ran over to meet Detective Franklin. "Her purse was on the ground. But she's gone. She's gone!" Ruth both screamed and cried. "I just went back in to get my keys ..." Ruth couldn't stop crying.

Detective Franklin put her arm around Ruth's shoulders while Sheriff McDougall talked to the patrol officers. "I need you to calm down and tell me exactly what happened."

Ruth Clarendon struggled to catch her breath. "Where could she be? The car door was open, her purse was on the ground, and she was gone!"

"All right. Let me talk to the other officers. Can you go into the shop and sit until I finish with them?"

Ruth nodded and went back to the bridal shop where the sales associates were all gathered outside the door. "What's going on," they asked. "Is someone hurt? What's happening?" Ruth could not answer their questions for all her crying. She simply shook her head, pushed past them, and entered the bridal store.

"Get me the security camera footage." McDougall barked the order to one of the officers as he scanned the doorways, looking for cameras. Of course, there wasn't a single security camera above any shop in Buffalo View Village. "Never mind." McDougall frowned and mumbled to himself. *Now what?*

Franklin told the sheriff on her way to her car, "I'm going to her house."

"Wait." McDougall stopped her. "Let me do that. Why don't you interview Boone and Grainger while I check out her house? If she's been taken, we need to know if either one of them is involved."

"You're right." Franklin looked into McDougall's beautiful blue eyes, "I think this is bad, very bad."

CHAPTER 17
Walter and Lorinda Stanche Are Up to No Good

A red Jeep Sport appeared directly in front of Ruth's car, driven by an attractive, older woman. The man who looked like Julian wrenched open the back passenger door, shoving Gloria inside the Jeep. He quickly zip tied her wrists and ankles and warned her again to keep her mouth shut.

"I've got nothing to lose and everything to gain, so believe me when I say I'll put you down like a dog and bury you next to my nephew if you utter one word."

Gloria did as she was told, all the while feeling panic breach her reason. She understood that her husband was dead. She didn't doubt the man. But what could he possibly want from her? All the recent chaos and upset led to this event, *but why?* She paid attention to where the driver was going. And she listened to every word they exchanged.

"Now what?" The man who was Julian's uncle sounded frustrated.

"I don't think anyone saw us, and if they did, they probably know what they saw, right?"

"Okay ...," the man replied, waiting for more from the

woman.

"The plan holds. We take her to her house, we fill her with pills, and we leave her to die." The woman ran a red light.

"Jeesus Lorinda! Watch it!" The man shouted. "Pay attention, dammit!"

Gloria realized they hadn't blindfolded her because she was not being kidnapped for a ransom. These two meant to kill her and make her death look like a suicide. *Is this what happened to Julian?* Gloria's mind was alert and on fire now, racing to figure out how to get away. She was grateful that Charlie Boone kept up with stalking her every move. *He'll see them take me in the house. But will he know what they're up to?* She felt a flutter of hope, panic subsided a little.

The driver pulled into Gloria's driveway. She looked up and down the street to see if there was anyone she could signal too. The street was quiet today and there was no sign of Boone's car. Panic rose again in her chest. Gloria felt lightheaded, as though she might pass out from fear.

Julian's uncle opened the back passenger door, reached in to snip the zip ties from her ankles and warned her again about the loaded gun he had ready for her if she so much as whimpered. Just then, Hank Broden rounded to the front of the house from the back. He offered his broken front tooth grin.

"I was jes here finishin' up. Looks like ye got yerself some company today, so I'll come back tomorrow, and we kin settle up." He looked Gloria straight in the eye and winked. "I got ye covered, Mrs. Stanche." With that he tipped his hat to Gloria's captors and went on. She could hear him whistling as he walked away.

She didn't notice that Broden's truck wasn't parked in the street or anywhere within sight for that matter. She didn't have time to wonder. Julian's uncle Walter—she'd learned her captor's names from the car-ride conversation—grabbed her arm and shoved her toward the front door. Lorinda, a step ahead, used a key to open the door.

It was getting on in the day, maybe 4:30 or so, and The Cat was well ready for Gloria to come home and fill his bowl. He was headed for the front door when Lorinda stepped inside the house. He turned tail and ran upstairs to hide in one of his many hiding spots.

"Nice house," Lorinda uttered. "We'll get a good price for it." As Lorinda inspected the house from attic to basement, Walter sat with Gloria in the living room.

"There's one way out of this for you." Walter spoke while he zip tied her ankles together again. "You can tell us where the money is." Gloria remained silent, afraid he'd shoot her if she spoke. "Tell me where it is, and I won't kill you."

"You told me not to talk."

"Smart ass, are ya?" Walter sneered at Gloria. "Talk now. Soon enough you won't be able to, and we'll inherit the lot anyway."

"I don't know what you're talking about." Gloria was confused and terrified. "What money? The money my mother left? There isn't that much, but you can have it if you'll leave me alive and alone."

Walter laughed. "Your mother! Ha! That murdering bitch!" Walter became agitated. "No. The money left for Julian from his boyfriend, Dorian Greene."

"What?"

"Which what? Your mother the murderer or Julian's boyfriend?" Walter was impatient.

"I don't know what you mean. Who did my mother kill? And Julian," Gloria's lips and voice quivered, "he was a philanderer, but with women!"

"You're not that naïve. Grainger filled us in on

everything."

Gloria was sickened by what they were saying. She fought against the gag reflex in her throat and the rumble in her belly. "Larry Grainger?"

Walter spat at Gloria's face. "Grainger. Did you really think he wanted to marry you for your middle-aged good looks? He knew about the money. He's the one who ..." Walter trailed off as Lorinda entered the room.

"There's nothing here that I can find." She glared at Gloria. "Where's the money? How do we get it? You're out of time, lady. We get the money, or you get to die. Your choice."

~~~~~

Hank Broden had been in the backyard, laying out some lattice work to paint, waiting for Mrs. Stanche to get home and approve the colors, when he heard a car pull into the driveway. He rounded to the front of the house to let the visitors know that Stanche wasn't home. He saw the elder couple, he saw the mean look on their faces, and he did indeed see the zip ties on Gloria's wrists. And he heard their gruff talk.

Hank Broden wasn't the smartest man, but he was no dummy either. He made nice with the thugs and passed them by, continuing down the street until they entered Stanche's house. He called the police. His call was relayed, not to Detective Franklin, but to Lorde who was still smarting from being kicked off the case by his former partner. He'd have his revenge and a payday, too, if he played it right. Now, thanks to that stupid house painter, Lorde had a mitt full of aces.

Broden told Lorde what he'd seen and promised that he would stay put until the police arrived. "You don't need to do that, Mr. Broden. I'm on my way right this instant. Great public service from you today, sir!" He couldn't see Broden puff with pride but was certain he did and knew he'd have Broden's loyalty if needed.

Lorde parked his unmarked car in the back alleyway, walked through Gloria's beautiful gardens, and using his own entrance key, entered the back door. He did not remove his shoes but wiped them quickly on the porch mat to avoid marking the floors with shoe prints of mud or other dirt. Gloria nearly fainted away with relief upon seeing the detective enter her living room.

"Where are we at?" Lorde asked the captors. "Did you find the money?"

Gloria's heart sank again. "Detective, why …"

Lorde glared at Gloria while interrupting her question. "Well?"

Lorinda sidled up to Lorde, pressing an ample breast against his arm. "We don't have anything." She frowned and stepped back from Lorde. "You're going to have to make this look like a suicide. There can't be any suspicions or none of us gets anything. Remember, there is 70 million on the table."

Gloria gasped. "I don't have 70 million of anything!"

"That's right. You don't. And won't until Julian's body is found. But we know where he is. Once you're gone, well, trickledown economics come into play. Morton will inherit everything."

~~~~~

Hank Broden, observing Detective Lorde, using a key to enter the house from the back, raced to his truck, and sped to the police station. It was a lazy day with hardly any traffic, foot or vehicle. He arrived at the station in record time.

"There's a bunch of 'em and they're gunna kill her," he shouted as he pushed his way into the station lobby. "Hurry!"

~~~~~

All three conspirators pushed and shoved and dragged and did whatever they needed to do to move Gloria, in full resistance, upstairs and into her bed. Walter continued to threaten her with the gun. Lorinda pulled a bottle of pills from her pants pocket and went into the bathroom to fill a glass with water.

"Get a few down her and give them a little time to work their magic. Then she won't be such trouble." Lorinda barked her orders to Detective Lorde. "Walter and I have to make sure the downstairs doesn't look like we were here. Come on, Walter. I'll need your help."

Lorde attempted to get the first pills into Gloria's mouth and down her throat. It was nearly impossible without help from the others to hold her still.

"Dammit," he exclaimed. "Get back up here and help me!" He shouted to Walter and Lorinda, but they were long gone, not wanting to be implicated should anything go wrong with this part of the scheme.

Lorde bent over her body and held her head with one arm and hand, while prying open her clenched jaw. "There!" He was triumphant. He was able to get three pills into her mouth before she bit him through the flesh. He screamed.

"You bitch!" He turned his head to hold his bloodied finger and inspect the damage.

Gloria, ever the quick thinker, raised her arms, still secured with a zip tie at the wrists and brought them down over Lorde's lowered head, bringing considerable strength down across his neck. There she held him, using every bit of body power she could muster. For the first time in his life, Detective Lorde was not happy with his face buried deep into a woman's cleavage.

He thrashed, attempting to escape her hold on his neck.

Droplets of blood from his bitten finger flew about the room. Gloria attempted to raise her body to a sitting position, hoping, to exert further pressure on Lorde, but that was a mistake. As she shifted, Lorde pushed himself further into her body and slipped out from under her arms. She was helpless again and exhausted.

Lorde went in search of a bandage. "You move one muscle, lady, and I will beat the living daylights out of you."

Gloria didn't care about the threat. He was going to kill her anyway. If he beat her, she wouldn't look like a suicide victim. She prayed as she'd never prayed before. "Father in Heaven, help me!"

Lorde heard her plea as he reentered her bedroom, a box of bandages in hand, and laughed. Just as he began to berate her about how God couldn't save her now, he tripped over The Cat who raced from under the bed. The box of bandages went flying from his hand as he struggled to keep balance. But he fell. He fell hard. His head hit the edge of Gloria's dressing bench as he collapsed, unconscious and bleeding.

Just then, Lucille called for Gloria from the base of the stairs and sirens came wailing to a stop in front of her house.

~~~~~~

Lorinda and Walter arrived at Larry Grainger's farm in time to see Detective Franklin exit her car parked near Grainger's house, next to his truck, at the end of a long driveway. Lorinda drove past the entrance and pulled over about a half mile down the road.

"Now what?" She asked, not expecting a helpful answer from Walter. "We have to shut him up, but maybe it's too late." Lorinda rested her head on the edge of the steering wheel.

"Maybe we should get away while we can." Walter was not helpful.

Lorinda turned her head to give him a sour look. "No. They don't know anything about our involvement unless Grainger says something. Maybe he won't talk."

Just then, Lorinda and Walter heard the sound of a police car siren coming from behind. Lorinda looked into her rearview mirror to see the flashing lights moving in the opposite direction from where she and Walter were parked. Lorinda revved the car's engine, did a quick 180-degree turn, and sped back toward Grainger's farm. Larry stood outside, next to his truck. The dust hadn't settled from Detective Franklin's hurried exit from his property, so he didn't have a clear view of who was driving toward him. He didn't have time to flee before Lorinda stopped the Jeep directly behind the farmer's truck.

"What did you tell her?" Lorinda screamed at Grainger.

Walter jumped out of the Jeep and onto Larry who hadn't had an instant to process what was happening. Walter was no match for the muscular younger man. Larry knocked Walter down and gave him a good hard kick in the side.

"You people need to calm down!" Larry shouted back at Lorinda. "I didn't tell her a damn thing. I didn't even know she was here." Larry glared at Lorinda. "And I don't know why you're here either."

Walter groaned as he tried to get up from the ground. Lorinda ignored him.

"We need to keep our stories straight!"

"There isn't any story for me anymore. Stanche isn't going to marry me. I'm not going to inherit when you kill her. Morton is your last hope and I hear he's already in jail. So, get out of here, now!"

Walter got to his feet and held his side with one hand while he shook his free fist at Grainger. "You bastard!" Walter reached for his gun, but it was gone. "Oh crap! My pistol is gone!"

CHAPTER 18
Franklin and McDougall Hatch a Sting

"You might want to get over here. I've got my former partner in custody for attempting to murder Mrs. Gloria Stanche. And that's not all." Detective Franklin clicked off from her call to Sheriff McDougall. She filled her coffee mug at the station coffee counter and entered her captain's office.

"How is she?" Franklin asked the captain who'd been monitoring, by phone, Mrs. Stanche's condition at the local hospital. "She's all right. No harm beyond the odd bruise and scared. Geez. That woman is a fighter!" The captain shook his head and smiled. "If I was twenty-five years younger and single..." His words trailed off as his phone rang. "Okay, thanks." He looked up at Franklin. "He's awake."

They rode together the few blocks to the hospital. There was hardly enough time to exchange thoughts but for one. "I don't want you questioning Lorde." The captain pulled into the hospital parking lot.

"Understood." Franklin was relieved. "I'll look in on Mrs. Stanche."

"And when McDougall gets involved, remember to keep

clear boundaries about your territories. We don't want to screw this up."

Franklin was in full agreement. "We've talked about this all along. We're good. He stays in his yard. I stay in mine."

"On the case." The captain finished with a wink. Franklin blushed. Every time McDougall met with Franklin at the Buffalo View Village police department building, she endured endless razzing by all the other officers, especially from envious female officers. A few of the men were equally captivated by McDougall's stunning looks and manner.

"Yes, sir!" Franklin turned her back on the captain and entered the hospital. At the reception area she asked for Gloria's room number, took the stairs to the third floor, and walked down a short hallway to Mrs. Stanche's room. Franklin was relieved to see a fellow officer on guard. She nodded to him and gently knocked on the hospital room door.

"Mrs. Stanche," she spoke softly as she slowly entered the room.

"Oh, come in. Come in!" Gloria was fully dressed and slipping on her shoes. "They're sending me home. I'm no worse for the scare of it all!" Gloria was flushed with excitement. "Your partner nearly killed me!"

Franklin walked up to Gloria and gave her a hug. "Unprofessional, I know, but I am so relieved that you are all right!" Franklin stepped back.

"Me, too! I thought it was lights out for sure! My cat saved the day." A nurse arrived with a wheelchair to take the patient downstairs. Gloria waved her off.

"It's hospital policy." The nurse objected.

"Whatever. I want to feel my feet under me if you don't mind." Gloria took Detective Franklin's arm. "Take me home."

"I really can't do that, Mrs. Stanche. If you're up to it, I need to take you to the station and get your story down for my report."

"Fine. It's amazing, really. Did anyone get Julian's uncle, Walter, and his woman partner, Lorinda?"

Franklin stopped walking. "What about them? What do you know about them?"

"They're the ones who kidnapped me and ordered your partner to kill me."

Just then, Franklin's phone rang. "Give me a minute, Mrs. Stanche. I have to take this."

The call came from the forensics lab about fingerprints taken off a loaded pistol found in Gloria's bedroom. "Walter Stanche."

"Okay. Thanks." Franklin looked at Gloria. "There was a pistol found in your room after the officers arrested Lorde and took you to the hospital. The fingerprints were Walter's. So, we have proof that he was there." Franklin was downcast. "I am so sorry this happened to you."

At the station, Gloria gave a complete statement about absolutely everything she experienced and heard from Lorde, the Stanches, and even from Hank Broden. "I don't give that man enough credit! He saw exactly what was happening. I will forever be in his debt!"

"We've already taken his statement. He's a real hero!" Franklin smiled at Gloria. "You're lucky to have good people in your life."

"Did I hear something about a local hero?" A stoutly built, middle-aged man dressed in khaki pants and a yellow knit polo shirt, stuck his head into Franklin's office doorway.

"Excuse me, sir, who are you?" Franklin began to rise up out of her chair, but before she could move in front of Mrs. Stanche to protect her, the man smiled an affable smile and backed away.

"Lester Hill is my name. I'm the publisher of the new Buffalo View Village Daily Reporter. I've come to introduce myself to the department and here I stumble on a hot story right outta the gate."

His smile was enchanting and his manner disarming. Gloria took notice and watched as Franklin guided the man away from her office to the reception area. "Please make an appointment with our captain." Leaving him with the officer at the reception desk, she returned to Gloria.

Just as Detective Franklin was about to close her office door against the curious and intruders, she spied Sheriff McDougall heading her way. She signaled him to enter her office and closed the door behind him. "Sit over there, would you? Mrs. Stanche, you remember Sheriff McDougall, right?"

Gloria nodded that she did and smiled at the sheriff. "Wait until you hear this," she exclaimed. McDougall pulled his chair closer, and Gloria began to describe once more in detail everything that happened to her that day. "And I know now that Julian is dead. Walter Stanche knows where to find his body. He told me that."

Detective Franklin and Sheriff McDougall looked at one another. "I'm still waiting to hear from the lab about the hand bones found under your bush. My guess is they were planted, likely by Morton Stanche. We are certain that Walter, Lorinda, and Morton Stanche were in cahoots. Their plan was to scare you into a state of such terror that it would seem credible you would commit suicide." Franklin rubbed her face. "We still don't know why."

"For the money." Gloria sighed. "All that money."

"What money?" Franklin and McDougall were caught off guard.

"You don't know about the money?" Gloria had forgotten to mention that small detail in her statement. "Once we find

Julian's body, I'm set to inherit seventy million dollars."

~~~~~

Before leaving the station, Gloria called Lucille to ask if she would be at Gloria's house when she arrived.

"They wouldn't let me come to the hospital. Are you okay?" Lucille sounded frantic.

"I am. Put the coffee on and maybe add a little Bailey's to it. I'll tell you everything." Gloria hesitated. "I hate to ask this of you, but would you stay with me tonight? And don't let me forget to have a security system installed in my house."

"Absolutely! I'll see you shortly." Lucille's romantic notions for Gloria were put away for the time being. Gloria needed her friendship more than she needed romantic advances, and Lucille was intent on being the best friend Gloria could ever have.

Lucille had the coffee brewing when Gloria entered the front door brushing past Lucille's outstretched arms available for a long hug. "I have to get a locksmith out here asap!"

"What about Hank Broden?"

"Of course," Gloria uttered. "You know, he was the one who saved me from that murderous bunch today." She called him immediately.

"I did not know that. It's all so horrible, Gloria. I still can't believe it happened to you or to anyone in the village." Lucille responded. She located the Bailey's, poured a shot in two cups, and filled them with fresh coffee. "We may need a few cups of this!"

"Thanks!" Gloria took a sip as the phone continued to ring. "Voicemail," Gloria said in frustration. "Mr. Broden, I am alive and well thanks to you. Please come by as soon as you can. I want to thank you in person and also ask that you change the locks in my house."

Just then, both women heard someone enter the house through the front door. Gloria froze. All color drained from her face.

"I'll go to see who it is." whispered Lucille who quietly crept forward toward the living room. "Mr. Broden!" Lucille exclaimed at the sight of the handyman.

"Yes, ma'am. Hank here. Jes changin' all the locks fer Mrs. Stanche. Everybody's got a key to this place, I tell ya."

Gloria jumped up from her chair to greet Broden. "Please, come in and have some coffee with us. Please!"

Hank Broden declined her request. "Well, I thank you, Mrs. Stanche, but I wanna get these locks done before my cousin gets here. He's gunna put in a fancy security system for ye. We can't be havin' all this calamity around here." Hank shook his head. "No, we jes can't." He looked up at the two women. "Good to see ya home, Mrs. Stanche. Good to see ya." Broden went about the business of installing new locks as Gloria and Lucille retired to the kitchen.

"How do I thank that man?" Gloria told Lucille how clever and quick Broden had been when her captors tried to get her in the house. "There was no one else around. No cars. No pedestrians. Not even a dog barked. It was eerie. And here came Hank, from the back of the house, as cheerful as can be. When he winked at me, my heart fluttered. I was certain he could see that I was in trouble. But then he was gone down the street and those thugs, they dragged me into my house and threatened to kill me." Gloria asked for another shot of Bailey's. "And hope was gone."

"Gloria," Lucille took Gloria's hand in her own stared her in the eye, "what did they want from you that was worth all this?"

Gloria wanted to tell Lucille about the money and about where it came from and why, but she hadn't thought the information through. She hadn't felt it through. It felt private and shameful. So, she didn't tell her the full truth. "They wanted money. They thought I had money."

"Why would they think that?"

"I … I don't want to talk about this anymore, right now. Is that all right?"

Just then, The Cat appeared and jumped into Gloria's lap. She pulled it to her face and smothered him with kisses while he purred and, like any cat when he'd had enough attention, squirmed to get away. "This one saved my life as well." Gloria set him on the floor. "If it wasn't for my cat, I'd probably be dead right now."

The two women walked out into the garden and sat on the iron bench by the bubbling fountain. The Cat followed and proceeded to lay down under a lilac bush. His tail leisurely twitched as the women gazed through the gardens and absorbed the calm of the summer afternoon.

~~~~~

Detective Franklin's phone rang. She looked up at the sheriff and smiled. Clicking off, she told him, "We've got the forensics back on the hand bones from Stanche's yard."

"Where did you find them?" Sheriff McDougall had not let on that he didn't know what Franklin was talking about during Mrs. Stanche's interview.

"I never told you? Are you sure?" Franklin seemed frustrated. "We went back to Mrs. Stanche's house after she called to tell me that there was blood on her bush before the red paint spill. I took a team with me and they sampled everything. They didn't find any blood, but they did find bones from a hand under the bush."

"So, whose hand is it?"

"The bones belong to Julian Stanche. Now we know he's

either dead or walking around without a left hand."

"No blood on the bush though?"

"Nope, but there were drops of blood on some of the bones."

"Do you know whose blood it was?"

"Cow's blood. Obviously meant to further the ruse of the severed ring finger." Franklin thought a minute before continuing. "I think we know that Morton Stanche set this in motion with the urging, I imagine, of Walter and Lorinda."

"Why now, I don't know, but I think he was done waiting to get Mrs. Stanche out of the way. And when his plan backfired, he met with the others to plot her end. That's when we found the three of them together in your county."

"I hadn't thought of it that way." McDougall looked thoughtful. "How are we going to get the Stanches? And shouldn't you pick up Grainger? Didn't Gloria Stanche say he was involved?"

"I've got officers out at his farm right now." A scuffle and commotion could be heard outside of Franklin's office. An officer knocked on the door and opened it to announce that he had Grainger in custody.

Detective Franklin stood to question Larry Grainger. "I need to get started on this guy, but I want you to listen in. Maybe he'll know where Walter and Lorinda got off to."

Larry Grainger was eager to tell all as long as he was guaranteed a shorter prison sentence in exchange for information. "I don't know where the money was coming from. They told me Gloria Stanche was set to inherit a huge fortune and they needed somebody to marry her, kill her, and inherit in her stead."

"And you agreed to be that guy?" Franklin sounded as disgusted as she felt.

"Well, yeah, but that was a long time ago. I figured they

scrapped the plan because I didn't hear anything more from them. The years went by and I thought now was the time to see if I couldn't get close to her. Maybe there wasn't any money. I wanted to find out."

"You thought now was the time and that time coincided with the appearance of Morton Stanche and his aunt and uncle, Lorinda and Walter, and all the chaos and terrorizing they brought into Mrs. Stanche's life."

"Well, I can see how that looks but, yeah, it was a coincidence." Larry Grainger did not appear to be lying however, Detective Franklin didn't believe him.

"And they were about to pay you a visit when I pulled into your farmyard this afternoon. Weird coincidence, that, too?"

Larry squirmed in his chair. "Yes! I swear it was the first I'd seen of them since they approached me with their plan. They showed up at my house to warn me to keep my mouth shut about them. I told them to buzz off."

"I think you're going to have a tough time selling that story in a court of law. A jury of your peers is not going to warm up to you one bit."

Franklin had an officer take Grainger to booking. As she left the interrogation room, she remembered that MacDougall had heard everything.

"We need to find them and nab them." McDougall was angry. "Now."

The two returned to Franklin's office to hatch a sting operation that would, they hoped, capture Walter and Lorinda Stanche. They put together a list of possible charges and left the Buffalo View Village police station together.

CHAPTER 19
Stung Like a Bee

Charlie Boone knew Jillian Grove the moment he saw her in that red Jeep pulled over on Barry Road, just past Grainger's place. He drove by her until he was out of her range of sight, then turned around and approached with caution. With excellent timing for him, a police car sped out of Grainger's driveway and up onto the highway as Charlie neared close enough for Jillian to see him. Not that she'd recognize him, he surmised. She wouldn't remember a nothing fella like him.

Jillian swung the car around and drove into Grainger's driveway. Boone pulled off the road so he could see any interactions with the farmer but was somewhat shielded by the tree line. Grainger still outside, was agitated with Jillian and her cohort. With arms flailing about in wild gestures, he appeared to be shouting. Grainger shook his fist and seemed to spit at Jillian as she and the other guy got back in the Jeep. Jillian turned around and raced out of the dirt drive, throwing up a dust storm behind her.

Boone followed her to the used car lot in town. He knew for certain that Jillian was behind all of Gloria's troubles. He didn't know the how or whys of her involvement, but he was unshakeable in the belief that she was bad news for anybody.

He watched as the couple, all smiles and laughter, walked the lot with a salesman. It didn't take them long to select an alternate vehicle and take it off the lot for a test drive. Charlie suspected they would not return the SUV, at least not willingly.

He followed Jillian as she headed for the highway out of town. The highway was nearly empty but for the two vehicles. Anybody who worked out of the village would be home by now, lusting for a satisfying dinner after a long day of office work or labor.

By 7:30, Jillian turned off the highway to park at a roadside diner. Boone was itching for her next move. He watched them eat burgers and fries and drink lemonade as they sat across from each other in their diner booth. Jillian was frowning and fussed with her fries, picking them up, putting them down. The pair didn't talk much. Just before 8:15, a sporty black Cadillac CT6-V, zipped into a parking space furthest from the front door. A man in his early sixties, dressed in black athletic gear finished off with blinding white shoes, bounced from the car, shadow sparring, then closed the car door.

Jillian looked up as the stranger entered the diner. He dragged a chair to the booth where Jillian and her companion were sitting, sat in a straddle, and began talking through a grin.

Boone could see the stranger slide a large manilla envelope across the tabletop to Jillian. She opened the flap and pulled out a packet of papers. She nodded and slid a much smaller envelope toward him. His grin was wide as he swung a leg over the chair, stood up and was gone with a swagger. He tipped his cap and grinned at Boone as he walked by. Once settled into his flashy car, he revved the engine and tipped his cap again. Boone didn't have time to wonder about the stranger's behavior, *probably high on something*, because Jillian was heading out of the diner without her partner.

Boone got out of his car and approached Jillian as she was about to step into the SUV. He pushed her forward through the open door and warned, "Don't scream. Don't yell. This will all be over soon." He deftly slapped a length of duct tape over her mouth. As she kicked at him, he caught her by the ankles, then whipped out a zip tie to hobble her.

Jillian continued to kick at Boone but missed him entirely as he was now on the other side of the car climbing in. He secured her wrists and pushed her head down as her partner left the diner from the opposite door. Boone slid out of the car and crouched at the back end, out of sight. When the man opened the passenger door, Boone tackled him from the back and secured him in the same way he'd wrangled Jillian. Satisfied with his work, he pulled out his phone and called the police.

In his earlier life, Charlie Boone had been a police captain and retired into private investigation work. He'd kept himself fit, even after he quit taking clients. He was a regular at the Buffalo Bodies Training Gym. He was well known and respected by the county sheriffs in his regions. When he called the Sacred Hope County Sheriff's department to report that he had in his custody suspects in a kidnapping case, he was patched straight through.

"Give me Sterling Jasperson. Tell him it's Charlie Boone on the line and urgent." Though his captives were well secured, Boone was impatient to hand them over to law enforcement.

"Well, Boone, ya old man, what've you got for me?" The sheriff was the son of a high school buddy of Boone's. Charlie had known him since birth.

As Charlie explained the situation to Jasperson, police car sirens screamed in the distance. "That was fast!"

"What'd ya mean?"

"Squads are pulling in at the diner right now."

"That wasn't me, but you've got yourself a couple of kidnappers. I just got an alert on those two!" Jasperson clicked off.

Just then, two Federal agents exited their vehicle with guns drawn while two other teams stood back, all with weapons aimed at Boone. His hands went up over his head. "These are kidnappers I've got tied up in the SUV. Sheriff Jasperson will tell you. I just got off the phone with him."

The first two officers approached Boone slowly. He didn't move but he did keep talking. "They kidnapped and tried to murder someone from Buffalo View Village. You can call the captain there for further verification."

While he talked, one of the officers circled to his back, pulled down his arms and zip tied his wrists. "I appreciate your cooperation, but you need to be quiet now. My detective will be here shortly."

Boone nodded in acknowledgement but spoke one last time. "They're still trying to kill her, Mrs. Gloria Stanche."

The young officer kneed poor Boone and took him to the ground. "Sorry old guy, but I told you to stop talking."

Sheriff Jasperson swung into the parking lot of the diner with lights flashing and sirens blaring. He pulled to a stop in front of the arresting officer, leapt from his car, and ordered him to stand down. "Get that man to his feet and make sure he's okay. Cut the ties. And leave him alone!"

"I can't do that, sir. I have to hear it from my superiors." The young officer brought Boone to his feet.

Just then, Jasperson felt a slap on his back. He spun around to find a familiar face. "What are you doing here?"

"This is my case." Dean Bridger, Jasperson's former partner, flashed his ID.

"This is Federal?"

"Yep."

"I know this man," he pointed to Boone. "I've known him all my life. He told me he apprehended," Jasperson looked around, "over there, those two. He said they kidnapped somebody and planned to murder them."

"I'm not surprised." Bridger looked at the kidnappers being escorted to separate black, undercover cars. "We had a sting going to get those two. I'll question your guy and send him home if I can."

Sheriff Jasperson approached Boone and spoke to him through a partially open car window. "You stepped in something here, a Federal sting, so you'll have to go with them. But I vouched for you. You should be okay. Call me if there's any trouble."

Both Boone and Jasperson knew he'd be taken to Great Gulch for processing. It would be well into the early hours before either of them knew anything. "Hey, Bridger, let me know when he's released, will ya?"

Jasperson stayed until the last officer was dispersed. He'd sent his guys home after he talked to Bridger. He entered the diner, sat down, and ordered a hot beef commercial with coffee. He chatted up the server, a petite, bleached blond, and tattooed female with one of those nose rings that always made him want to wash his hands.

"What happened in here tonight?"

"I'm not sure. That's what I told that Federal agent." The server looked confused. "There was hardly anybody in here. I guess it was the man and woman seated over there." She pointed to the booth where Jillian sat with her partner. "And this other older man came in, pulled up a chair at their booth and made himself comfortable. He was a flashy sort and cocky from what I could see. Swaggered, you know?"

Sheriff Jasperson nodded. "And then what?"

"Well, he left. Then the woman paid and left while her

friend went down the hall to the restroom. Then he left. That's all I know." She looked over her shoulder to the order counter. "I was back there, cleaning the grill most of the time." She grabbed the coffee pot just as Jasperson's order was ready.

"Order up!" The cook didn't look at the server or Jasperson.

"What about him, does he know anything?" Jasperson held out his mug for her to fill.

"He probably knows everything. He's the type that sees all and keeps his mouth shut to all. He's seen the inside of a prison and isn't looking for a repeat."

The server placed Jasperson's meal on the counter with utensils. "Napkins are there. Salt. Pepper." She left him to eat while she wiped down tables.

"Sheriff Franklin, she around?" Jasperson called the Buffalo View Village PD before loading his fork with mashed potatoes, brown and greasy with gravy.

"It's important. Call her." He clicked off the phone and finished his food. It was cold in the diner and the Muzak versions of pop tunes annoyed him. But he was hungry and stayed until his plate was polished clean with the last of the white bread.

"Thanks." He handed the server cash. "A receipt?"

Jasperson left the restaurant and started his car, then looked around before driving. *What in the hell happened here?* He turned onto the highway and headed north. A few miles down the road a highway sign informed him that Great Gulch was 165 miles ahead.

~~~~~

Charlie Boone was getting tired. An early riser, he'd been up since 4:30 a.m., at the gym, then sleuthing on behalf of Gloria Stanche. He watched her leave her house around eleven with Ruth

Clarendon. Odd combo he thought. But then he remembered the girl was set to marry the Blue Fox kid. *Maybe she needs a mother type with her.* He followed them to the bridal shop then left to run personal errands. He knew she'd be fine for a few hours.

"I can't believe I left her to fend for herself. Dammit!" His mumbled words were to himself mostly. He was in a dark, windowless Federal interrogation room. "I should have kept with her, but I didn't know Jillian Grove was involved." He sat back in an uncomfortable chair and closed his eyes. He was snoring when Bridger woke him up.

"Here." Bridger pushed a cup of coffee toward Boone. "This shouldn't take long. We know who you are. I don't know why you are in this particular mix of thugs and shysters."

Charlie laughed. "Me either!" He took a swig of coffee. "Thanks. What time is it?"

Bridger ignored his question. He too was tired. His daughter's sixteenth birthday clocked in about two hours ago. He should be home with his family, sleeping, and fully rested for the birthday trip in eight more hours.

"How do you know Jillian Grove?"

Charlie relayed all the relationship information he had going back to his high school years. Jillian was the woman who snatched Gloria's father away from Bethany Lee. How he despised her. He had no idea she was in town or what she wanted with Gloria.

"But when I saw her out at Grainger's place, I knew her instantly."

Bridger stood, coffee cup in hand, and prepared to leave. "Jasperson's here to take you back to Buffalo View Village."

"That's it?" Boone was stunned.

Bridger walked out the door without a word, passing by a young agent assigned to process and escort Boone out of the building. On the three-hour drive back to Buffalo View Village, Sheriff Jasperson told Boone what he knew of the story, including Jillian's alias, Lorinda Stanche.

"Well then who in hell is Julian Stanche?"

CHAPTER 20
Jillian Grove

"Where are we going to find those two?" Franklin muttered aloud. She was driving to a used car lot on the edge of the village. As soon as she and McDougall got in her car, a call came through that the red Jeep Sport had been spotted there. "They may have left something in the vehicle. They're probably rattled because they know we have Walter's gun."

"Maybe. I'm guessing they aren't done with Mrs. Stanche yet, though. There is a lot of money left on the table. "And they are the only ones who know where Julian's body is."

"Right. Without the body, they can't get the money."

"They won't kill her though. Not now. They'll find some other way to get at the money."

"Yes! And I think I know exactly what they'll do!" Franklin pulled into the used car lot and drove down the center aisle to park directly behind the red Jeep.

The owner of the car lot was expecting them and was ready to help in any way he could. "Yeah. They took me, for sure. Stuck me with police property, right?"

"It is now," said McDougall who reached for the vehicle keys in the lot owner's outstretched hand.

"What did you sell them?" Franklin was inspecting the Jeep's exterior as she questioned the owner.

"I didn't sell them anything. They took a Toyota RAV 4 for a test drive. I've got ID from one of 'em." He handed a driver's license to Franklin. The name on the license was Jillian Grove, not Lorinda Stanche. She glanced at the photo, then took a second look.

"Thanks. Not her."

"Not her, who?" The owner looked as if he might cry.

Just then, a tow truck arrived along with a patrol squad and two officers, to haul the car to the police impound lot. "Thanks guys," Detective Franklin peered into the open driver's side window of the patrol car. "I'll check back later for your report."

Franklin and McDougall got back into her car after giving the lot owner instructions on how to file a report. "Sorry I can't help you with this right now."

The lot owner, head low and fuming, yelled at his staff. "Meeting. Now!"

"We're headed to Stanche's, right?" McDougall clicked his seatbelt into place.

"Right."

~~~~~

Gloria thanked Hank for his heroic actions earlier in the day and for securing her home against further intrusions. She bristled at his inference that she had been lax with security.

"Don't ye be givin' keys or codes away, now."

She held her attitude back. "I don't know how anyone got those keys, but I assure you, it wasn't nor will it be, from me."

Hank tipped his hat as he left the house. "See ye in the morn 'bout the trellis colors."

"I'd forgotten! Yes. Thank you. About ten?" He nodded,

climbed into his old but well cared for work truck, and headed for home.

Gloria closed the door behind him and turned to Lucille who was in the kitchen cooking dinner. "I'm suddenly hungry. I've not eaten since I had hors d'oeuvres at the bridal shop this afternoon. The kidnappers did not stop for a light meal!"

Both women erupted into laughter. They laughed themselves to tears, breaking the tension of the day into small bouts of gleeful relief. When Lucille was able to catch her breath, she finished making dinner.

"I made French toast with strawberries and if you've got any whipped cream I think we should drown our food in it. Comfort food. That is on the menu tonight!"

The kitchen smelled wonderful. The Cat appeared for its meal. "Let's eat outside. I'd like to enjoy the evening air." Gloria filled The Cat's bowl on the porch. Just then, Detective Franklin and Sheriff McDougall strolled into her backyard from the alley.

"What are you doing here?" Gloria dropped her fork, set her tray on the iron bench, and stood to greet Franklin and McDougall. "And why are you sneaking into my yard? Are they back? What's happening?"

Lucille took Gloria's arm and hand. "You're all right, Gloria."

Detective Franklin spoke first. "I'm sorry to upset you. I promise you that this ordeal is nearly over. I would like you to take your things into the house. We'll come with you and explain everything."

Lucille and Gloria picked up their dinner trays and headed toward the house. "Cat, come!" Gloria called for The Cat who stayed where he was under the lilac bush. "Once you all are out of sight, he'll come." She didn't sound sure of it, not one bit.

"I'll make some coffee." Lucille was already filling the pot with water. Gloria measured coffee grounds into the filtering basket of the coffee maker.

"I'd like us to meet in the living room, Gloria. We'll pull the drapes." Franklin and McDougall closed the heavy curtains in the living room and turned on two small table lamps for light.

"Here, let me." Lucille slid the coffee tray away from Gloria whose hands were shaking. "Go sit in the living room with the officers and find out what's going on. I'll be in when the coffee has brewed."

Gloria nodded, wiped her hands on a kitchen towel, and patted Lucille on the shoulder as she left the kitchen. "I feel like I'm going to die tonight."

"Nonsense!" Lucille was stern. "You have the entire village on high alert. Nobody will get near you."

Gloria was silent as she settled in her reading chair. She looked first at Detective Franklin and then at the sheriff. Then she closed her eyes.

"I know you're scared, but really there isn't anything to be afraid of anymore. We know what they're going to do next and we're ready for them." Franklin's words were measured against Gloria's panic. Panic was winning.

"How can you know that? How can you know anything?"

Sheriff McDougall took the lead. "We know they won't give up because of what you told us about the enormous amount of money you've got coming to you. But we know about them, right? So they can't hurt you. They have to do something else. And that will be to have you sign bogus papers, giving them the rights to Julian's inheritance."

"How would that happen?"

Franklin sat forward in her chair with an almost eager look on her face. "We're certain they plan to drop in on you this evening, probably while you're sleeping and scare the living daylights out of you to get you to sign whatever papers they bring."

McDougall jumped in. "But we'll be here. We're staying overnight with you and your friend to ensure that absolutely nothing goes wrong. We have officers watching the house from every angle. This will be done by dawn. I promise you."

"My cat!" Gloria interrupted. "I have to bring in my cat."

Detective Franklin followed her to the porch. "Please stay back. I want to make sure he comes in the house and doesn't run." Gloria called for The Cat who sauntered toward her, entered the cat door, and sat at its bowl for a drink of water. Gloria blocked the cat door for the night.

"Mrs. Stanche," Detective Franklin and Sheriff McDougall stood side by side. Under normal circumstances, Gloria would have noticed what a fine-looking couple they made. But these circumstances were extraordinary. She was scared and fitful. "We're going to stay in the kitchen so you two can have privacy. We are a whimper away so try to relax. We're right here."

"You don't need to do that. I'd prefer it if you would stay with us. We can play cards. Do you play cards?"

"Thank you, Mrs. Stanche, but our job is to keep you safe. It will be better if we are together in the other room. Remember, there are undercover officers surrounding your house."

Gloria gestured to Lucille. "Come sit with me."

"Shouldn't we clean up in the kitchen first?"

"Oh, of course. What was I thinking?" Gloria stood and all four walked into the kitchen.

Gloria loaded the dishwasher while Lucille put away the uneaten food. "Have you eaten anything?" The officers shook their heads. "Gloria, let's make pizza. I saw some Italian sausage in the freezer. I know you have mushrooms and cheese."

"I have my canned tomato sauce in the pantry downstairs.

I'll get it."

"No, ma'am." Sheriff McDougall was quick to stop her. "Tell me where I can find it and I'll go."

For a minute, Gloria had forgotten her terror. Now it came rushing back. "You don't think they're in the basement, do you?"

"I do not," he assured her. "But I don't know that they aren't. I'd like to check it out."

"Gloria, let him be. Where's your yeast?"

As the yeast bubbled in warm water, Lucille mixed the other ingredients for the dough. Detective Franklin watched her every move. "I've never made dough. It looks easy."

"With practice," Lucille smiled, "it is."

McDougall returned with the tomato sauce. "All clear. That basement is spotless. You made my job easy!"

Gloria showed her pride with a warm smile. "It's a lot easier, I find, to keep things clean as I go, than to clean up messes I've left for later."

"Amen!" Lucille laughed as she spread the pizza dough on an oversized baking sheet.

The air filled with warmth from the oven and smells from the baking pizza. Lucille set the kitchen table. Gloria's fears bubbled up and subsided, then bubbled up again. The Cat rubbed against her leg when she sat down to eat.

"It's odd, I suppose, but I feel comforted by my cat. He already saved my life once today."

Lucille took her hand. "Let's pray over this food and ask the Lord to keep us all safe, especially your cat!"

McDougall laid three slices of pizza on his plate. "Sorry ladies, but I don't know when I'm going to get another meal and this, this looks spectacular."

"Stand down, officer!" Franklin admonished the sheriff as he reached for a fourth slice. Her smirk bordered on flirtatious.

"The troops need to eat, too!"

Everyone tried to initiate small talk, but Gloria could not be swayed from her panic. She offered her pizza slices to McDougall.

"You will eat!" Lucille was adamant.

After the meal, Lucille and Gloria cleaned up the kitchen then retired to the living room. "I can't tell you how much I appreciate your friendship." Gloria looked as if she might cry. "You've been through so much with me in these last weeks. I really thought it was over." And then the tears came hard. She gasped for breath as her chest heaved. She couldn't talk. Lucille threw her arms around her and held her close, thinking more of Gloria's needs then her own desires.

She rocked Gloria and stroked her hair as if she held a frightened child in her arms. "Here," she handed Gloria a box of tissues. "Dry your eyes. And you know, it's getting late. Let's get you upstairs and to bed."

"I'm not going up there!" She raised her voice. "I'm staying down here with the police. And so are you. This is a sleeper sofa. We'll open it up and sleep here if we can sleep at all."

Gloria was the first to rise in the morning. "Oh, my good Lord," she exclaimed out loud, "I'm not dead!" The living room was still softly lit by the end table lamps. Franklin and McDougall were gone. She woke Lucille. "I don't know where they are." Gloria was afraid all over again.

"If something were wrong, they would have alerted us. I promise you. Check your phone."

Lucille crept into the kitchen, not convinced that what she'd said to Gloria was true. The kitchen was as they'd left it last night. She started the coffeemaker.

"Oh, Lucille! You were right! Detective Franklin left a message that the Stanches were arrested late last night!"

The smell of the coffee brewing, the sunlight brightening

the room, the sound of Lucille in the kitchen taking cups from the cupboard swept her with an overwhelming sensation of peace. "I'll feed The Cat." On her way through to the porch with The Cat at her ankle, she mused to herself that this would be a wonderful day.

~~~~~

Early into the morning, at two a.m., Franklin's phone rang. Both officers, still sitting in the kitchen, reacted, each on high alert. "They what?" Franklin paused. "He what? I'll be there as quickly as I can." Franklin clicked off. "McDougall, we've gotta roll."

"What's going on?"

"They were picked up last night out in Oakville. Boone caught 'em."

"Boone?"

"Yep. And he got nabbed by the FBI."

"What?" McDougall stammered, "what, what, why?"

"We're about to find out."

CHAPTER 21

Lester Hill Learns the Truth

"It's been a long time, old friend." Lester Hill shook Roland Blue Eye's hand. "Nice office you've got. Can I sit?" Lester pointed to an oversized, comfy-looking brown leather chair draped with a red and white striped Pendleton blanket. "Nice blanket."

Roland, a handsome man by any standard, kept his thick black hair, long and loose. He was a traditionalist and since he was not married or involved, he did not braid his hair, but kept it pulled back with a leather tie. "Gift. Yeah, you can sit there."

Rather than sitting behind his desk as though meeting with a client, Roland sat in a facing chair of similar design. The two were separated by a polished stone-top table. Hill stroked the surface of the table. "Nice."

"Have some water."

Hill ignored the tray with water pitcher and glasses. "I'm good." He sat back in the chair, a hand on each arm and looked up at Roland. "I'm here."

"I see." Roland chuckled. "And you brought the newspaper with you?"

"Per your request, I opened a newspaper business in Buffalo View Village, the Buffalo View Village Daily Reporter. Is there really enough news around here for a daily?"

"There will be." Roland poured himself a glass of water and drank it down. "We've got a local story about to break open that will put us on everybody's radar. I wanted somebody I trust to write it."

"As I recall, you were the one who breached trust!" Lester chuckled as he gazed around the office space.

Roland laughed, revealing a startling bright smile. "I remember you as being honest, at least for a white guy. But I admit, pranking you with that girl and her father could have left you suspicious of my motives."

Roland's mood became more serious. "I've been following your career. When I saw that you were about to retire and sell your paper, well, the timing is just too good." Roland smiled again, sitting back in his chair, relaxed and confident, with one leg up over the other. He was always one for cowboy boots and these, handmade and deep maroon in color with silver accents, were highly polished works of art.

Lester snorted. "Don't forget, my grandmother who raised me was part Lakota. I don't know which part, but maybe the honest part."

"Maybe." Roland rose from his chair and walked across the room to slide a prairie landscape oil painting to one side. "This is my personal safe, disguised, not by the painting that hangs over it, but by the large safe that sits out in the open behind you."

He unlocked the safe and withdrew a large packet, closed the safe, then sat down again to face his friend. The packet lay on the tabletop between them.

"You want me to touch that?"

"I do."

Lester Hill reached for the envelope, opened it, and slid the contents out and onto the stone table. "This looks like a police file." Lester sorted through the pile of documents and photos. "So, who are these people?"

"That one is Edgar George Buford. I manage his estate. He died six weeks before this man," Roland thumbed through the documents to lift a photo of Julian Stanche. "He left a substantial fortune to Julian with the caveat that the estate would be available to Julian's heirs at the time of Julian's interment."

"What?"

"Right. So, Buford and Stanche were a couple and had been for most of their adult lives. Actually, Julian and I were a couple in high school. He left me for Buford." Roland smiled. "That was a long time ago."

"I always suspected you secretly wanted me." Hill snickered. "But why the caveat?"

"Never!" Roland chided Hill. "The caveat. Buford wanted to be as certain as humanly possible that Julian would not be murdered by fortune-seeking family members."

"You said he was married?" Lester took notes as Roland spoke.

"Yes. To Gloria, who frankly has grieved the loss of her husband all this time."

Lester looked up from his notepad. "Who would be on your list of potential murderers?"

"There's a long list of family and other grifters who knew about the money."

"The wife?"

"She did not know and as a result has recently been attacked by Julian's family — mother, father, and twin brother — in a scheme to terrorize her into suicide."

"You've lost me." Lester Hill sat back in his chair. "Take another run at this."

"Right. So, Julian's body was never found. It is believed

that he died in a boating accident. However, I know that he was murdered. All three of them know he was murdered. One of them witnessed the murder. I don't know which one, but they say they know where Julian's body is buried. Buried is dirt, ground, not water, lake." Roland took a breath. "Even if they didn't witness the assault, they know someone who did. And all three are in custody as of this morning."

"For what?" Lester looked again at his notepad.

"Kidnapping. I don't know the rest of it."

"Okay. How do you *know* Julian was murdered?"

"I was told by the local handyman. He was hired to install a garden fountain at Gloria's home – then her mother's house. He wasn't certain, but there was evidence of blood on a shovel which he gave to me for safe keeping. Just in case. He'd placed the water pipes the day before and came back to pour a concrete slab for the fountain and hook it up."

"Who did he say killed the guy?"

"I don't know that yet, like I don't know whose blood is on that shovel."

Lester looked surprised. "Why haven't you gone to the police with this?"

"Because even though I suspect a lot, I really don't know anything. That's why you're here."

Lester frowned. "I'm supposed to investigate this story of yours?"

"No. We've got a local retired P.I. who has been shadowing the widow – the daughter of his high school sweetheart, I think – and he just nabbed the mother and father who kidnapped Gloria yesterday afternoon."

Lester was flabbergasted. "What?"

"She's okay. But the plan was to kill her and make it look like a suicide. Their plan nearly succeeded from what I hear. Then they would inherit, after somehow revealing the spot where Julian's body resides."

"Is anyone else involved?"

"I don't know. You'll want to talk to Charlie Boone, the old P.I., to see if he knows more."

~~~~~

Lester Hill called Gloria after leaving Roland's office.

"Oh, yes," Gloria's face flushed red. "I remember you. We met at the police station. You are the newspaper man, correct?"

"Why, yes. I'm flattered that you would remember me."

Gloria had noticed his pleasant round face, round as a planet, and his head as bald as a boulder. She could tell right away that the twinkle in his eye was a natural phenomenon, not practiced with intention to entice and deceive. And, she noticed, he was built to last - muscular and tall, over six foot two, she thought. Yes, Gloria most certainly remembered Lester Hill.

"Of course. What I can I do for you?" She hesitated, then sighed. "I suppose you want to talk about all that's happened to me recently."

"I do. I'd also like to take you to lunch. We can talk then."

"I can't meet you until two o'clock. Is that all right?"

"Whatever works best for you, Mrs. Stanche, works best for me."

Gloria's heart was pounding, and not because she was panicking about reviewing the terrifying episode of yesterday, or any of the awful things that had been the focus of her life of late. No. She had not felt excitement for another man, not outside of her dreams, since Julian. Now that she knew for sure Julian cheated on her, not with women, but with one man in particular, her grief lessened. Her longing for him was all but gone. She felt compassion for him, realizing that his life with her must have been lonely. But she was angry too. *What a terrible way to treat someone! To take my love and use it to cover up his own love and leave me with nothing!*

Dressed in a blue and white striped tailored shirt dress and canvas slip-ons, Gloria entered the Shamrock Grill and Steakhouse. She didn't often wear makeup, but today, she added a little color to her face, wanting to accent her well-shaped lips and hazel eyes. Lester Hill was waiting for her at the restaurant entrance.

"Mrs. Stanche," he greeted Gloria with outstretched hand, grasping hers in his large palm. As he closed his fingers over her much smaller hand, she flushed.

"Mr. Hill."

"Oh, call me Lester, or Les. Everybody does." Hill led her into the restaurant and signaled to the hostess they would be a party of two. With his hand at the small of her back, he gently guided her to a booth near the back of the restaurant. "Please, sit."

Gloria slid into the camel-colored booth. The table was white with gold flecks. The waiter handed each of them a menu and set tableware and napkins to the side.

"The dining room doesn't open until six o'clock, so I hope the lunch area is all right." Hill thanked the waiter for menus and asked for water with lemon slices for both of them.

Gloria smiled at Lester. "This is fine. I've always liked this restaurant. They have the best chicken salad."

Gloria set her menu down and found Lester Hill staring into her eyes. She flushed red, again. His eyes were brown, ringed in black. She lowered her lashes to break the stare.

"Mrs. Stanche," Hill began. "I've spoken with my college buddy, Roland Blue Fox. He told me what he knows of your story. I have some questions to ask of you if you don't mind." His voice seemed sincere. "I don't want to publish anything you are uncomfortable with. As a reporter though, I have to disclose that I might, if I feel those details are necessary."

"Call me Gloria, please." She sipped her water. "Until I hear your questions, I don't know what to say about that."

"Fair enough."

The waiter arrived to take their orders of chicken salad with a fruit bowl and fries.

Gloria placed her napkin on her lap and sipped water, while Lester took his first bite of chicken salad. "You weren't kidding! This is great!"

"Yes. I can't do better. By the way, I did speak with Roland about you after you called me."

"I must have passed muster or you wouldn't be here, right?"

"You did. I am curious though about the newspaper. Where is it? I don't recall a publisher in town for many years."

Lester followed a handful of fries with a swallow of lemon water. "You don't need a printing press any longer, Gloria. It can all be done online. I hired a couple of college journalism students to keep the website current and I'll add my bits as they come along. It's mostly a lark."

Lester paused with the last forkful of chicken salad hovering near his mouth. "I sold my paper in Stapleton last year so I could retire and travel. Then Roland called a couple of weeks ago and asked if I would come here to cover your story and make sure it was published and sent out to my contacts." He finished his salad and the last of the fries, then started in on the fruit bowl.

"Why is Roland so invested in what's happening in my life? He never did explain himself when he warned me off telling the police anything more. I'm glad I did not heed his warning. Although one of the officers was involved with my kidnapping and would have murdered me."

"What?"

"I don't understand yet what happened. Detective Franklin assured me that she would fill me in once confessions were signed and filed."

"Would you like to take a walk and tell me what all happened?"

Gloria nodded, wiped her mouth, finished her water, and left to take a walk with this stranger to tell him as little as possible until she knew more about his story and if he could be trusted.

~~~~~

Charlie Boone agreed to meet Lester Hill at Stomper Bar on the outskirts of Buffalo View Village. He ordered a beer and nibbled on peanuts while he waited for the newspaper man to arrive. Charlie always showed up early. He liked to have time to scope out the surroundings before meeting a client, or in this case, a reporter.

When Hill walked in, Boone stood up to greet him. "Over here." He waved Hill to a stool next to his at the bar. "Another one for my friend here."

"Thanks." Hill took a seat and had a good look at Charlie Boone. Old. Fit. Good natured?

"I checked you out with the village P.D. just to make sure you were legit." Boone shelled a peanut.

"Good. Okay then. You are willing to talk to me about the Stanche case?"

"As much as I can. I'll tell you what I know. My full name, by the way, is Charles Kelly Boone, for when you publish the story."

CHAPTER 22
Larry Grainger Spills the Beans

"Mr. Grainger." Detective Franklin sat opposite Larry Grainger in the Buffalo View Village Police Department's one and only interrogation room. "Can I call you Larry?"

"Why am I here?" Grainger protested. "I have a farm to take care of!"

"Well, Larry, as you know, there's been a lot of trouble made for Mrs. Gloria Stanche lately. Your name comes up. I want to find out why and then maybe you can get back to your farm work."

"That's simple. I'm a friend of Gloria's and we are both members of the Buffalo View Village Garden Club. That's it."

"My notes say that you were present in her home late one evening, uninvited I imagine. This was reported by a neighbor who saw you enter, furtively, they said. That's the word they used."

"I explained that to Gloria. I was concerned for her

wellbeing. When she didn't answer my calls or texts, I went by her house. The door was unlocked, and I entered to check on her."

"Mr. Grainger, Larry, I need you to be honest with me. I know that what you just stated is untrue. Let's start again and with the truth please."

"I am being honest. I have nothing to hide. I don't know where you're getting your information from, but it's wrong if it says I'm lying."

"Let's try this again. On the day that we were interviewing Mrs. Gloria Stanche in her home, in her own living room, you entered her home without invitation. You were surprised to see us, correct?"

"On that day, you are correct. I entered Gloria's home, and as I've told her many times, I was there to check on her, to make sure she was okay."

"And yet, sir, before you noticed us sitting in the living room, you had already placed a foot on the first riser of the stairway leading to the second story of her home."

"Are you trying to set me up for something? I didn't do that."

"You forget, Mr. Grainger, that I was sitting across from the entryway and the stairway. My view was unobstructed and yes, you behaved as I described."

Larry squirmed in the uncomfortable metal chair. "Okay. Look. I didn't do anything. They wanted me to do something but that was a long time ago and I didn't agree to it."

"And who is they?"

"The Stanches. Julian's parents."

Just then, there was a knock at the interrogation room door.

"We're busy."

The door opened to reveal Franklin's captain framed in the doorway. He gestured for her to follow him.

"I'll be back." Detective Franklin left the organic farmer alone in the room with no windows and no way out. He picked at a bit of soil stuck under a fingernail and tried to listen for sounds of someone coming back to question him further. The room was silent but for his own breathing, his boots shuffling back and forth, and the fingers on his right hand, drumming on the tabletop.

~~~~~

"What is it, sir?" Franklin was led into the captain's office.

"The Feds are releasing the Stanches and Lorde this afternoon. I'm sending a team to bring them here. Too bad about Lorde. He got caught up with some bad people."

"I feel bad for him, a little. But he was willing to kill somebody, so whatever he thinks his motive might have been, there was something else going on." Franklin kept her hand on the doorknob, eager to get back to questioning Grainger. "He was just about to tell me Lorinda and Walter's scheme when you interrupted."

"Will he tell the truth?"

"I think that's where we are now, sir. He began by lying, but now he knows he's caught, so whatever he knows, I think he's ready to tell. Probably will want a deal."

On her way back to the interrogation room, Detective Franklin glanced at Detective Lorde's desk. It had been cleaned out and was waiting for a new occupant. A chill ran through her body. *He will never be back. He'll be an old man before he's freed from prison.* The realization that Lorde had given up everything for the hope of wealth and maybe even for revenge saddened her. His crimes were terrible but still she felt compassion for her former partner.

~~~~~~

As Detective Franklin entered the interrogation room, she found Larry Grainger slumped over the table. He stirred slightly when he heard the door open.

"When will she be back here?" He mumbled into his arms at rest under his chin. "And can I have some coffee or water?"

Franklin signaled to an officer before entering the room. "Get this guy some coffee, will you, and a bottle of water?"

She closed the door with more force than was needed. "Let's start from the beginning, the first time you met Lorinda and Walter Stanche."

Grainger straightened up. "It was shortly after Julian disappeared. Maybe a week? Not sure."

"How did they contact you and why you in particular?"

"They lived here when the boys were in high school. Well, Lorinda did. Walter was off somewhere working, I guess. I suppose Julian told them I was having some financial trouble then, just converting my first farm to organic. It wasn't going well."

"So, what did they offer you?"

"It was pretty simple, really. They wanted me to marry Gloria Stanche. They said she was set to inherit a decent insurance settlement once Julian was legally pronounced dead. They wanted a percentage, that was all."

"Really?"

"I guess. I'd always liked Gloria, so it seemed like not such a bad idea. But then as time went on and Julian's body wasn't found, Gloria wasn't getting over him."

That's not really what happened, is it?"

Larry reached for the water bottle and took his time screwing off the cap and taking the first swallow. He did not look Franklin in the eye. He set the bottle to the side, put his hands under the table, and rocked slowly back and forth in his chair.

"Mr. Grainger. Quit stalling."

"Some of that is right. But after so many years, Gloria Stanche caught my eye again. I don't even remember what she did or said. Nine years is a long time to get over somebody. I thought it was time. It was time for me."

"That's a nice story but it doesn't explain why you were in her house, twice, when you thought she wasn't home."

Grainger began rocking back and forth in his chair again. His face drained of color. "Okay. Okay. Julian's body wasn't found. Okay? But I'd heard about another inheritance, a big one. I wanted to look for papers or something that would prove she had big money coming."

"How did you hear about it?"

"They came back and told me their plan. They still wanted me to marry her, but there was more. I overheard Lorinda talking to Walter when they thought I was out of earshot. They planned to murder Gloria, make it look like a suicide. Then they were going to sic the police on me, say that I killed her for the money."

"So, there was money to inherit?"

"Turns out, Julian was gay. I didn't know that. Anyway, he'd been involved with an extremely wealthy man who died and left his estate to him. But there was a caveat. In the event of Julian's death, the estate could only be given to Gloria after Julian's interment. I guess he wanted to make sure that she wouldn't kill him for the money. But I guess he felt guilty too. Anyway, that's what I heard them talk about."

Detective Franklin stood up and glared at Larry Grainger. "You knew this and didn't tell us? What's wrong with you?"

"Hey, do I get a plea or immunity or something for telling you now?"

"Do you live behind the eight ball?" Detective Franklin,

furious, left the interrogation room, signaled to a nearby officer. "Take that man back to holding. And get me Charlie Boone!"

~~~~~

Charlie Boone, freshly showered and shaved, though short on sleep, arrived at the Buffalo View Village Police Department around 11:30 that morning. "I'm here to meet with Detective Franklin."

He sat in the waiting area which was mostly empty but for a weeping woman and a young girl with her left arm in a cast. The girl tried to console the woman who was now sobbing. "Look, Mom, I'm the one with the broken arm, for Pete's sake! That stupid boyfriend of yours, well, I'm glad he's gone!" The woman cried louder.

Charlie wondered at the messes people got into because of love, then nodded to himself. *And here sit I.* He thought about his feelings of love for Bethany Lee and for the first time wondered why he'd kept at it so long.

"Mr. Boone? Follow me." A middle-aged officer signaled for Boone to follow and led him into the interrogation room, shutting the door with a solid click of a lock, leaving Boone alone to wait. His wait was short.

The door opened within minutes. "Coffee?" Detective Franklin extended a styrofoam cup toward Boone.

"Thanks." Boone sat back on the uncomfortable wooden chair, at ease as he lifted the lid from the coffee cup and blew on the steaming brew.

"I understand you had a long night. You know you could have spared yourself that if you'd called us."

Boone nodded. "I could have, but when I saw Jillian Grove, all sense went out the window. I had to know what she was doing here. I had a pretty good idea she was behind everything that was happening to Gloria Stanche."

"Who is Jillian Grove?" Detective Franklin sat straight up, wearing a look of total amazement, having expected to hear the names of Lorinda or Walter or Morton Stanche.

Boone recounted his experiences of the day and night before in detail, relishing the story himself.

"Jillian Grove. I've seen that name somewhere. Wait!" Franklin's face lit up. "She's Lorinda Stanche?"

The wheels began to turn in Franklin's mind, churning up the clues and putting them together like a jigsaw puzzle. She excused herself and left the room, leaving Boone with his coffee and silence.

She knocked on her captain's door. "Yeah?"

"Captain. I've got it. The couple in custody with the Feds – Jillian Grove – that's an alias for Lorinda Stanche. So, the gist of it is that they were playing a long game. After nine years, they schemed to terrorize Gloria Stanche, pushing her to an emotional edge, then kill her and blame the murder on somebody. First it was going to be Larry Grainger, the farmer, and ultimately the fall guy was Lorde. Although he would have been the murderer, right?" Franklin took a breath. "Morton would have inherited once they revealed, anonymously, where Julian's body was buried. That's the piece I don't have. I need Julian's body." She shook her head. "But Lorde got caught attempting to murder Gloria Stanche. They couldn't inherit if he snitched. They needed something else. I'm guessing the kids in that photo we found at their house are related, nephews maybe. I'll bet they're next on the list should Gloria Stanche die. They may not even know anything about the scheme. They'll just be the next victims." Franklin shuddered. "Even from prison, they'll try to find a way to get that money."

The captain was thoughtful. "Time will tell. Hopefully. I

suppose you'd better find those kids – maybe they're grown men by now – and make sure they are not involved and fully informed. By the way, I got a call from Roland Blue Fox a while ago. He tells me he has the answers we're looking for. He should be here any minute."

On cue, Roland appeared at the Captain's door, carrying a large manilla envelope and garden shovel wrapped in plastic. "Before you try to arrest me, there's a reason I didn't come forward before. That reason is that I didn't know for certain that a crime had been committed. I received my information and this garden shovel, nine years ago, from the handyman, Hank Broden. He found the evidence. If there is blood, Julian's blood, on this shovel, then Broden can tell you where to find his body.

CHAPTER 23

What Happened to Julian Stanche?

It was nearly nine o'clock in the morning when the forensics team began to dig up Bethany Lee's fountain in her daughter's back yard. Gloria was distraught.

"You know they found Julian's blood on my mother's garden shovel." She spoke without inflection. There was no question to ask, only a statement of fact made to Lucille Persons.

"What are they looking for, do you know?"

"The rest of my husband, Julian."

Lucille stood with her friend in the porch, watching as police officers filled her yard with their bodies and their equipment to excavate Julian's bones. "Can I get you some tea or something to eat?"

Gloria turned to look at Lucille. "We may as well go inside. I don't need to watch the destruction of my beautiful gardens."

Gloria sat at the kitchen table while Lucille heated water for tea. She'd had a bad … was it a week, a month, how long since the trouble first begin? She couldn't remember.

Lucille brought cups and water and lemons and a selection of tea bags to the kitchen table. "Oh, I almost forgot! I'll be right back."

Gloria didn't notice or hear anything Lucille was doing or saying. Her grief billowed, pushing heartache to its limit. *My mother did this for money.*

"I still can't believe it." Gloria, emerging from despair, spoke aloud. "And so many people knew. All this time." She looked around the room. "Lucille?"

Just then, Lucille returned with a basket of freshly baked muffins. "I forgot these in the car. Would you like me to warm them?"

Gloria stared at Lucille, then nodded. While lemon peel and orange pecan muffins heated in the oven, Gloria stirred her tea. Lucille sat across from Gloria and smiled.

"I know this is a terrible day for you. But you know this brings an end, not only to the attacks against you, but all your questions will be answered."

"They are answered. My mother did this. She killed Julian and buried him in the backyard. Who does that in real life? It's so cliché!" Gloria almost smiled.

"Do you know why she did it?"

"I do. It was about money. This entire nightmare has been about money. A little bit of money. A lot of money. The possibility of money."

"I'm listening. I'm just going to take the muffins out of the oven."

The sugary aroma of warming muffins filled the air. "I swear, Lucille, your baked goods could lighten the mood in hell." Then she did smile. "I'll take one of each!"

"Tell me what you learned from Detective Franklin." Lucille placed a plate of warm muffins on the table.

"My mother – the mother I thought loved me – was involved in an under-the-table handshake deal with a couple of city council members. They think Julian found out about it and threatened to expose her if she didn't pull out of it. They argued in the garden. That part I know for certain because Julian's parents confirmed their involvement."

Gloria sipped her cooling tea and peeled a wrapper from an orange pecan muffin. "Oh," she inhaled the aroma. "This smells so good." She broke the muffin into bite-size pieces, relishing each one.

"I will admit if there's any one thing I do well, it's a muffin!" Lucille laughed and took a bite of her own.

"This is calming. Thank you. Thank you." She sat for a moment, listening to the commotion outside. The Cat was well hidden in the upper regions of the house. "By the way, I am set to inherit 70 million dollars." She popped another muffin bite into her mouth.

"What?"

"I know. Lucille, I have been grieving a man for nine years who was in love with a wealthy man who died and left Julian his fortune. But. There was a caveat. Julian's body must be interred before I can inherit. That's what this has all been about. Well, not Julian's murder." Gloria paused. "My mother murdered my husband and planted him in the backyard. I just can't wrap my mind around it."

Lucille patted Gloria's hand at rest on the table. "How could you?"

"He's under my beloved bridal wreath bush. Can you believe it? The irrigation system for the fountain? It runs right by it. Hank Broden installed it then came back once the ground had settled and planted the bush."

"I'm missing something here, I think."

"I know. I'm jumping around. It's a lot to digest." She added more hot water to her teacup as the voices outside grew louder with what seemed to her to be enthusiasm.

"My mother hit Julian in the head with a shovel and killed him when he confronted her. Hank came back the next day to finish up with the fountain and noticed what he thought might be blood on the shovel. I don't know why, but instead of calling the police, he took it to Roland Blue Fox for safekeeping. The police found Julian's hair and blood on it once Blue Fox turned it over to them."

"Why did he wait?"

"He claims there was no crime that anyone could prove so he kept it just in case there ever would be a crime discovered."

"What my mother didn't know, was Julian's parents – the people who kidnapped me –learned about the land deal and wanted in on it. They showed up at the exact moment she murdered Julian, stayed out of sight while she buried him in the irrigation trench Hank dug that morning. And they sat on that information all these years, scheming to rob me first of Julian's life insurance and then they learned about the seventy million dollars."

"Good Lord, Gloria!" Lucille was overcome with shock. She stood and began to pace. "This is horrible stuff!" Lucille's eyes were wide and her mouth gaping. "Your husband was gay. Your mother was a murderer. People you know knew these things for years and kept the truth from you. How can you be so calm?"

Gloria smiled at her friend. "What can I do? It's a relief to know now. I have been grieving the loss of my husband for nine years and now I feel almost nothing. That's good! The rest of it, as long as people are dead or going to prison and can't hurt me anymore? Well, that's good too!" Then she winked. "Besides, I've met someone."

"What? Who?" Lucille sat down.

~~~~~

The forensics team went to work digging up Bethany Lee's fountain and her cherub marker and all the pipes for irrigation. The last thing they pulled out of the ground was Gloria's bridal wreath bush. At Gloria's request, the fountain and the cherub marker and her beloved bush were tossed into a dumpster, along with the irrigation system, to be unloaded at the Buffalo View Village landfill. Gloria had already reached out to a local landscaper to help her design a new sanctuary space in her backyard, one that would obliterate any memory of the crimes committed there.

Julian's bones, minus a hand, were exposed and exhumed with utmost care. The process was overseen by the Medical Examiner and Detective Franklin. The forensics team had to be warned more than once to settle down and quit making so much noise – not from their equipment or forensic activities – but from their exuberance over solving a nine-year-old crime.

Later that day, the Medical Examiner confirmed that Julian Stanche died from a blow to the head with a shovel, Bethany Lee's shovel. Lorinda and Walter and Morton Stanche were all charged with kidnapping and attempted murder with a variety of other charges to be delivered by the Buffalo View Village District Attorney. No charges were leveled against Larry Grainger, the organic farmer, because he'd only considered a crime, not actually committed one.

The biggest surprise for Gloria came when she was told that the name, Lorinda Stanche, was an alias for Jillian Grove.

"So, Jillian Grove was Julian's mother? Why did she change the name?"

Detective Franklin took her time revealing this new information. Gloria had been through enough trauma. She didn't want this to be one more upset for Mrs. Stanche.

"Her last name changed, of course, when she married Walter. But she changed her first name because she was known locally. You may recall that she lived here when Julian was in high school. She left Buffalo View Village once he graduated, although they stayed in touch. She's altered her appearance sufficiently, so people didn't take notice when she returned. Except for Charlie Boone. He recognized her at first glance. And they weren't living here. They were in Mission County, which is how Sheriff McDougall got involved.

"Charlie Boone saw her? He didn't tell me."

"There wasn't time for telling. When he saw her, he followed her. That was right after you were kidnapped when they left Lorde to kill you. But he didn't know about that."

"He told me about Jillian Grove, that she took my father away from my mother who was pregnant with me. That was in high school." Gloria searched her memory. "I believe he said she came from a wealthy family so why did she need my money? And do you know what happened to my father? Is he Walter Stanche?"

"We learned that her father lost his fortune and she's been on the hunt for one ever since. This isn't the first scheme or scam she's been involved in. The Feds interviewed her about other crimes then turned her back to us for her crimes against you."

"And Walter?"

"We do not believe he is your father. You can request a paternity test if you want to be certain. For your sake, I hope he isn't. That could make Julian your brother."

"Those people are cold hearted enough to allow something that horrible. I mean, they witnessed the murder of their own son and did nothing but use that to blackmail my mother. The murderer."

~~~~~

As the forensic team finished up, Detective Franklin

knocked at Gloria's door. "May I come in?" Lucille met the detective at the entryway door.

"Of course. Please remove your shoes."

Detective Franklin sat on the porch bench to take off her shoes. Just then, The Cat entered the porch and began to rub against Franklin's leg.

"You know the commotion and madness are nearly over, don't you?" The Cat purred while Franklin stroked its back. She noticed the block to the cat door. "You'll have to stay inside until we fill in the trench. Sorry, buddy." Franklin stood and entered the kitchen.

Lucille handed the detective a muffin. "You probably didn't have breakfast."

"Thanks! I didn't." Franklin did not unwrap the muffin but held it while she updated Gloria. "We found his body and it's now in the care of our Medical Examiner." She scanned Gloria's face for emotion but there was nothing but a nod. "I have officers filling in the trenches, but you'll want to have someone else out here to fix the mess. It is a big mess."

Gloria smiled. "There's always a mess to clean up somewhere for some reason. Am I right?"

Lucille laughed and thanked the officer for all of her help and support. "Will you be attending the Village picnic on Friday?"

"I will."

"Bring that handsome sheriff with you."

Franklin smiled and thanked the women for the muffin, then left through the porch door with The Cat at her heels.

"Gloria, you started to tell me about someone you met. Did you mean a man?"

"Yes." Gloria blushed. "Lester Hill. He's new to the area. Roland Blue Fox asked him to come here to start a newspaper. He was going to retire, but Roland enticed him with the big story that's about to break – not about my kidnaping, of course, but the massive fortune."

"Oh, that's not good."

"I know. Roland and I have worked together to split the fortune among multiple charities. I don't need that kind of money. It isn't mine anymore, or won't be once the estate is probated, so nobody will come after me, hoping for a fortune."

"So, what about Lester, is it?"

"We're going to the picnic together. I haven't been this excited about something in a decade."

Lucille took the news as she knew she must. Her friend deserved love. A good love. She was happy for Gloria, truly happy.

CHAPTER 24
The Buffalo View Village Garden Club

"Is everyone present? Ginger, would you do the roll call please?" Gloria Stanche, president of the Buffalo View Village Garden Club for the last four years, was excited to be doing something other than worrying about who might want to do her harm.

"Quiet, quiet! This is a great day, I know, but we need to be quiet so I can hear your 'heres!" Ginger Spalding, short, stout, and bubbly, winked at her companion, Herman Edison. "Herman is here. Nancy, where is Francine?"

"She went back to the car to get the door prizes. We purchased two *Geum triflorum*, Prairie Smoke, if you don't know."

"Okay. Next? Paulette? Here. Larry? Larry? Anybody seen Larry?"

"He'd better not show his face around here!" Herman, usually soft-spoken and gentle was angry. "Gloria," he looked up at her, "I am so sorry about all that happened to you. We didn't know anything was going on until we read about it online."

Ginger added, "Where did the newspaper come from, anyway? I heard Cindy's kid is a reporter."

Gloria used her gavel to turn the attention back to roll call.

"Oh," Ginger sputtered, "sorry. So, no Larry. Next? Mitchell?

"Here."

"Karl?"

"Here."

"DeeDee, Mini, Zinnia and Doug. Where's Katie?"

"I'm over here." Katie was sorting glass flower vases near the exhibit tent that had yet to be erected.

"Gloria's here and I'm here, so that's that!" Ginger sat down.

"Would you all move into groups by committee? And Ginger, would you check your list to make sure we have all tasks covered?"

"Karl and I will put up the tent since Grainger is gone. Katie, wanna help?" Mitchell smiled at Katie Spain, gesturing for her to join the men in erecting the exhibit tent.

Katie, the local florist and like Gloria, a widow, was shy but blossomed with encouragement. "Of course." She joined the two men and began sorting spikes and ropes.

Meanwhile, Hank Broden, though not a member of the garden club, had volunteered to paint the lattice work panels that would be placed behind exhibit tables and was unloading his truck. Paulette Jensen scurried to help him.

"Great work as usual, Hank." Paulette often employed Hank to assist her in creating sculpture pieces and to package artworks for shipping to galleries and customers.

"Thank ye!" Hank seldom smiled. He didn't need to. His pleasant, helpful nature was obvious in his every move.

"You know that you are the town's hero, right?"

Hank did not respond but kept loading latticework panels onto a flatbed cart.

"Seriously, Hank, what you did to help Gloria was heroic.

You saved her life, and you solved the mystery around Julian's disappearance."

Hank, without acknowledging Paulette, loaded the last panel onto his cart and pushed it forward to the exhibit tent, now upright and ready to accept exhibit tables.

"So grateful you've come to help," Nancy Barry warmly welcomed Hank. "These panels look beautiful. How do you plan to install them?"

The question was rhetorical as Hank had already begun to pull long metal spikes from a bucket on the cart. He began to pound them into the ground, through a series of two-hole straps he added in threes on each panel end. The red color as backdrop against the white tables was striking. Katie, with Nancy's help, set the exhibit placards in place that included each exhibitor's name and plant variety to be displayed.

The tent was open on three sides to allow the summer day's breeze to flutter through. Everyone hoped that the weather would be this perfect for tomorrow's picnic. Gloria and Lucille, with the help of Douglas Walker, brought individually prepared lunches and had them ready for the club members when the village bell chimed at precisely twelve o'clock noon. The day before, Hank installed a handwashing and plant watering station behind where the exhibit tent would be erected. Club members joked about being in the clean hands crew.

"Just like our mothers always told us!" Mitchell showed his hands to everyone. "Not a bit of dirt under these nails and I dig in the dirt for a living!"

"Oh, you do not!" Karl complained. "You manage the crew that digs in the dirt. Your hands haven't touched the ground since your promotion. Now these," Karl raised his hands for all to see, "these are dig-in-the-dirt hands."

Zinnia Walker was the next to raise her hands. "These

hands helped to create award-winning dahlias. And these hands," she lifted her husband Douglas' hands, "have helped create stunning new iris varieties." She pumped their joined hands as if in victory. "Dirt is good!"

"Soil is good. Dirt is dirt!" Herman piped in.

DeeDee scooped watermelon balls into her mouth. "It's all the same to me as long as it produces spring lilacs and summer roses." She gave Herman a look of challenge. "Don't start!" Then she laughed. "Lucille's mixed berry pie is the only reason I stay in this group!"

There was a chorus of amens followed by a brief moment of silence as each garden club member chewed their first taste of lunch and sipped lemonade. It wasn't long though before the chatter started in a low mumble.

Mini Jensen was the first to whisper to her aunt Paulette a bit of gossip she'd heard about Gloria Stanche. "Was she really getting it on with that farmer, Larry?"

Paulette was incensed. She liked Gloria and from what she knew through the press and those who said they knew; Gloria had suffered enough terror and trauma. This should not be chased with embarrassment. Paulette, no stranger to brazen outspokenness, stood up and asked for everyone's attention.

"Listen up people. I know that this is the first gathering since our dear friend Gloria's tough times. So, let's knock off the gossip and rumor mongering and shadiness that I know for a fact is roaming about this table. If you have something to ask Gloria, do it. Otherwise, keep your mouths working on things that won't hurt her, like floral arrangements and tomorrow's membership drive!"

There wasn't a soul at the table who gave more heed to Paulette's opinions-as-barked than their own, but they didn't want to upset Gloria who stood still with a darkening expression. "Thank you, Paulette, for that. But I don't need protection any longer. I will for a thousand years be grateful to Lucille Persons, here, for her unyielding support while my life was in danger. And make no mistake, people meant to murder me. If you want to talk about that, go ahead, but don't do it around me. I have zero interest in hearing anything about that ever again. Are we done?"

Everyone was staring at Gloria and nodding in unison. A typically noisy group, they were as one in humbled silence. During the course of the day, each garden club member made a point of approaching Gloria with a personal apology and sincere demonstration of concern. As much as she did not enjoy their gestures, in some ways she was relieved. It was out in the open and could dry up and blow away instead of simmer to a boil later.

If anyone bothered to pay attention, they would see that Mitchell didn't let Katie out of his reach. Whatever task he undertook, he asked that she help him. Finally, after three years of waiting, he asked her for a dinner date.

"And how about a movie, too? What do you like?"

Katie smiled all day and beamed when he asked her out. "Yes," she said to dinner. "Anything but a horror film is fine," she said to a movie.

Some of the other exhibitors were also setting up tents, notably the police department and the new newspaper. Two college students, Sean McFee and Claudia Yorke, worked with the city electrician to get power and internet to their booth, shared with the BVVPD. No one else cared about electricity. The food vendors had their own generators, and the carousel power source was installed years ago.

Exhibitors were careful to keep to the sidewalk and other paved areas as much as possible. Everyone prided themselves on maintaining beautiful grounds for the picnic. Mini Jensen helped Karl place planters of geraniums and marigolds and petunias by resting benches and tables. Mini was meticulous in her plantings, adding alyssum and portulaca around the edges for more color and contrast.

Francine, in an unusually good mood because her boyfriend had been sober for two weeks, took pictures and videos of everyone working together, keeping the village citizens up to the minute on social media about the progress of this year's picnic set up.

At four o'clock, everyone was cleaning up their spaces. By five o'clock, when the city bell rang, Douglas and Herman wheeled out coolers of beer and sodas while the local chicken shack delivered platters of wings. At sundown, someone lit a fire in the firepit. People gathered after work, kids skateboarded on the perimeter sidewalks, and lovers found out-of-the way corners for handholding and kisses.

When the last straggler left for home, Gloria was already in hers, petting The Cat and musing about tomorrow's picnic, Ruth Clarendon's wedding, and having Lester Hill at her side. She was nearly asleep in her reading chair when there was a knock at her door. She hadn't yet closed the drapes and for a moment she couldn't remember if she'd fed The Cat.

"What time is it?" She mumbled out loud to herself as The Cat leapt from her lap. "I'm coming." Gloria was a little apprehensive, even though she knew everyone who meant to hurt her was in jail. She flipped on the outside light since it was approaching full darkness. "Why Lester! Please, come in!"

Gloria's heart pounded in a good way. "Why didn't you call?" She was surprised at his lack of manners.

"I did. A couple of times." He stepped into the kitchen and presented Gloria with a bouquet of gladioli. "For good luck in all ways tomorrow." His smile was gleaming.

Gloria was flustered and pleased. "This is so sweet of you. Thank you. Do you want some lemonade, or I have a beer, I think, maybe more than one?"

"No, thanks. I really just wanted to come by and wish you luck. I also wanted to say how pretty you looked today out at the picnic grounds."

"I didn't see you there!"

"I know. I stopped in to check on the kids setting up the booth and saw you with Lucille. You looked pretty. And I wanted to tell you that. And so, I have." With that, Lester Hill stepped forward toward Gloria Stanche and kissed her on the cheek. "Until tomorrow's picnic." He smiled, turned, and said goodbye.

Gloria closed the door behind him as if in slow motion. She couldn't remember the last time she felt like this. She crossed herself and thanked the good Lord for sending Lester Hill her way. She fed The Cat and let him outside. He managed to figure his way through the backyard, dug up as it was, so she felt no need to go out with him. The less she saw of that mess, the better she slept at night.

Back inside, Gloria closed up the house for the night. She pulled out a notebook that contained checklists for the picnic, for the wedding, and for the cleanup tasks after each event. The Cat came back in the house and plopped down at her feet. Everything was back to normal except for the flip flop of her stomach and her flushed face every time she thought about Lester Hill. She was a little worried that he might be interested in her since he knew about the fortune but not about the plan to give the money to charities. But she doubted Roland Blue Fox would have encouraged a relationship with Lester if he thought that Hill was a grifter.

Roland was as guilty as the rest of them for leaving her to suffer such deep grief for so long over a man who had never loved her. He apologized frequently, saying that he hadn't known what to do. But when he learned she was in trouble, he stood up for her.

"Did you? I don't recall that. I remember you coming to my

house, too late in the evening, to warn me off the police. I still don't know what that was about."

"I didn't want you to find out about Julian. Not until you had to."

"That is pure nonsense. You aren't a stupid man. You knew I was about to find out everything. After all, you had the evidence in your possession."

"I didn't know what I had. I wanted to hear from you if there was any reason for me to come forward. How was I to know the shovel had anything to do with what was happening to you?"

Gloria knew that was the best she'd get from him. Still, she trusted him with her inheritance. After all, he'd been managing it for nine years without siphoning a dime for himself. If he could be trusted with money, he could be trusted with love. Love always trailed a far second to money. She'd just learned that lesson for life.

CHAPTER 25
The Buffalo View Village Picnic

Lucille Persons offered up her mixed berry pie, strawberry pie, and orange pecan muffins for judging in the food tent. She could barely muscle her way through the swarm of her competitors with their freshly baked breads, cookies, pies, biscuits, and every manner of leavened and unleavened wheat flour-based goods.

The centerpiece of the picnic was the Elmore and Sylvie Blue Fox Memorial Exhibit where historical photos and notes of remembrances adorned the temporary tent walls and display cases. This was the hall of fame for Buffalo View Village families who had shown great love and devotion to one another throughout the year. Each year families vied to be seen as the most demonstrative in their love toward their kin. Those voted most loving would receive a sizeable wooden and metallic plaque, engraved with each family member's name. At the end of the year the plaque was returned to the memorial committee for display with all the other families acknowledged before them. Usually, the plaques were returned in fairly rough condition as families fought over who should have possession of the award. Built into the memorial budget were replacement costs, used every year but for two.

Notebooks of recommendations for the nominated families

lay open for picnic goers to inspect. Everyone except nominated family members could vote for their family of choice. These votes were tallied at the end of the day and added to the Committee's votes for a final decision. The award-winning family would be announced at the conclusion of the festivities. No one, not even the young people, left early. Everyone anticipated the outcome – some with dread, others with hope, some with confidence. There would be brawls in the night regardless, and everybody knew it.

Lucille and her husband, the Episcopal minister, were nominated for the most loving family award, along with several other families of note, one of which had won the prize three years in a row. Lucille felt terrible about the nomination. Afterall, she was not loving toward her husband though she vowed to do everything in her power to rekindle her former affections for him.

Gloria had braved the upheaval in her backyard to maintain what remained of her gardens. Her efforts produced Red Nordland potatoes, Bright Lights swiss chard, and Rosita eggplant to exhibit. She entered giant yellow snapdragons and colorful cactus zinnias in the floral competition.

She noted that the beer garden was already busy at eight thirty a.m. because they served up the best breakfast to be had of eggs and hash browns, sausages, and pancakes. The fine arts exhibit tent was managed by Paulette Jensen and featured local artists, to give many a first exhibit experience. Her niece, Mini Jensen, was as talented as her artist aunt, even more flamboyant and edgy in her paintings and sculpture pieces.

Gloria and Lester met at the beverage hub an hour before the festivities began. They sat together at one of the courtyard tables, watching in silence as exhibitors brought their items for judging.

"Should we take a walk by the tents and see what everyone has brought? I won't have time to explore the booths once the picnic begins." Gloria was dressed in a pale yellow, sleeveless shirt tucked into form-fitting denim shorts. She wore strap sandals instead of her gardening shoes, and her toenails were polished a blush pink.

"Absolutely. But be warned, I'm not going to let you work all day and not enjoy the picnic. And don't forget, at seven p.m., you need to be dressed and ready for the wedding. Although, you look lovely as you are." Lester squeezed Gloria's hand.

"Thank you! You look nice, too." Lester was wearing canvas slip-ons, blue shorts, and a tan striped shirt. Gloria appreciated everything about Lester's look and felt proud to be with him. More than any other thing, she loved the attention he gave her, the compliments, the small gestures, the remembering of things she said she liked.

"I'll be leaving at five thirty to change and be back here to help Ruth with whatever she might need." She squeezed his hand too and smiled while she blushed. "I'm happy to be spending this day with you. I haven't been on a date since high school. Back then, I had a crush on Roland. And then I married his boyfriend. How could I have been so unaware?" Gloria flushed with shame. "You realize, I hope, that as much as I'm enjoying the attention from you, it will be a while before I fully trust anyone. I can't apologize for that."

"Gloria, I'm in no hurry to move our time together into anything deep or dramatic. I'm new here, finding my way in this town and starting up a business. I plan to travel as much as I can. I like you, don't confuse what I'm saying. I like you a lot." Lester sat back a little in his chair and took a good look at Gloria. "I recognize that you have been in this village all your life with the same friends and one husband and then one dead husband for a long time. Suddenly your world blew up."

Gloria flinched. "Yes. And I don't want to feel bad about

taking time to reorganize myself, my thinking, my outlook."

"Good God, girl, you got back up after so many knockdowns, so fast, you absolutely need to take time. I'm sure the world looks vastly different to you today than it did two months ago."

"Honestly, I'm enjoying the calm of routine. I like my life. I've always liked my life. But I have tied a lot of it up with grief and that was a mistake. So, yes, I need to re-experience everything; find out what I like as Gloria Shifton, not the widow Stanche."

"You're changing your name?"

"As you know, my mother was a murderer who killed my husband over money, so it's not a name I'm proud of, but it is my name, not his name, so yes."

"Your resilience amazes me!" Lester relaxed and smiled. "I suppose we'd better get on the move or we won't have time to see anything before you disappear into the bowels of the horticultural exhibit." They stood in unison, each with a cooled cup of coffee in hand. "Gloria, I am going to kiss you." And he did.

Just then, Detective Franklin appeared in full uniform. A flustered Gloria waved her over. "Are you working today?"

"Hello, Gloria, Lester. I'm always working." Her laugh was light and sweet. "The picnic is a great day to teach kids about law enforcement. We always have free chili dogs and ice cream. That draws them in."

"What about Sheriff McDougall? Will he be here today?"

"Is someone talking about me?" McDougall, dressed in comfortable summer clothes, walked up behind Franklin, and put his arm around her waist.

"I didn't see you coming!" Gloria had been so focused on Detective Franklin she didn't hear McDougall or smell his aftershave.

"I'll see you later, Gloria. Glad to see you looking so

beautiful, rested, recovered!"

Gloria smiled as McDougall and Franklin walked away, his arm around her shoulder. "A lot of good came out of the bad, didn't it?"

Her question was rhetorical, but Lester Hill agreed. "Yes. You do look beautiful. Oh, you mean them?"

Gloria nodded. "Yes, they met because of my case." She paused for a moment, to think. "I like romance." She was matter of fact in this pronouncement, making Lester laugh.

"Me, too."

They parted company so Gloria could help in the horticultural exhibit tent. By the time she arrived nearly all the exhibitors had placed their items for judging.

"I'm glad I'm not a judge this year," she whispered to Lucille who was at the membership table.

"I'm with you. Everything is exceptional this year. Although, that floral arrangement with the coral tea roses and white Shasta daisies is spectacular."

Just then, two older gentlemen approached the membership table and asked for information. "We live out at the old Clausen mansion on Bridge Road. We moved there in May and are beginning a rejuvenation of the grounds. We'd like to join your garden club if you'll have us. We could host a meeting or two next summer."

Gloria excused herself from the conversation and joined Ginger and Herman at the vegetable display table. "You've managed to keep all the vegetables looking fresh. What did you do?"

Herman lifted red checked cotton towels that lined the bin for each entry. Underneath he exposed a bag of small ice cubes. "I replenish the ice as needed," he told Gloria, "from my cooler under the table."

"That's a great idea! When will you announce the winners?"

"During lunch," Ginger interrupted. "We're still undecided about a couple of entries."

Gloria nodded and moved among the other tables, asking if anyone needed help and listening to their stories of the day so far. When the noon whistle blew, she was not surprised to find Lester at her side, ready to lead her away for a lunch break.

"What do you want to eat?" Lester gestured toward the food vendor lane. "Hot? Cold?"

"How about a burger and fries with a side of coleslaw? Picnic food."

Lester left Gloria to place their order. She relaxed at her table and gazed out across the picnic grounds. "Is this seat taken?"

Gloria jumped at the sound of a man's voice but was met with the sunny smile and close-cropped chestnut hair of Sean McFee, the young reporter.

"Please, sit down. How's your mother?"

"She's fine. She's around here somewhere. Probably at the pie table. Listen, Mrs. Stanche, I wanted to say how sorry I am about all that happened to you recently. I'm learning the ropes as a reporter and I'll tell you I was shocked to learn how many deviants we had in Buffalo View Village."

Gloria couldn't help but laugh. "I suppose they are deviants. Good word choice!"

Just then, Lester arrived with lemonade. "You want some, Sean?"

"No. I'm good. I wanted to let Mrs. Stanche know that my whole family is praying for her."

"That's sweet, Sean. Please tell them I appreciate their prayers."

"Yes, ma'am." The young man reached out his hand to

shake hers. "That was some story!" Sean said goodbye and returned to his post at the newspaper tent.

Noisy laughter of children and adults, the whirring sounds of skateboarders, and the occasional outburst by someone disgruntled over something, made the early afternoon feel festive and communal.

"I do love this day I think, better than any other in the year." Gloria held the cool cup of lemonade. "Thank you for sharing this with me."

Lester winked. "Our order should be ready." He left again to retrieve their lunch.

Just then, Lucille sat down next to Gloria. "It's a beautiful, beautiful day!"

"It is. I was thinking the same thing. I wanted to call it perfect but didn't want to jinx it."

"My husband is bringing our food. Do you mind if we lunch with you?"

For the next hour, the couples chatted and laughed and soaked up the sounds and smells of the picnic. At one o'clock sharp, the judges began announcing exhibit winners in the various categories. Lucille made a sweep with her baked goods and Gloria was awarded Best in Show for her eggplant. After all awards were presented, the announcer asked everyone to wait for one more special award.

"This year, we would like to add an award. Our committee was unanimous in this. The new award will be called the Buffalo View Village Outstanding Citizen Award."

The crowd applauded this decision and each in his own mind began to contemplate how he might win next year. They reveled in the idea of another competition.

"Would Mr. Hank Broden please come to the podium."

There was silence in the park except for the skateboarders

who continued to whiz to and fro and attempting jumps and spins.

Hank made his way from the back of the park where he had been sharing a lunch with DeeDee Ahlmstad. He took off his cap and ran his hand over his head to present a neat and tidy mop of light brown hair.

"This is for your outstanding support of one of our most valued citizens when she was in dire need. You were recommended for this award by The Buffalo View Village Police Department and Mrs. Gloria Stanche. Thank you, Mr. Broden."

Hank Broden was never one for wordiness. In this moment, as he accepted the award, face flushed with humility, he could offer only a weak, "thank ye." He shuffled off the stage and was cheered by all as he made his way back to his lunch partner.

On his way he stopped at Gloria's table to thank her for this honor. She took his hand. "Hank, I want you to know that my gratitude is endless and forever. What you did, the way you handled yourself, that is why I am alive today."

Hank kept his head down and mumbled his appreciation, as his face grew redder, and his heart pounded furiously in his chest. "I jes wish I coulda done more for ye, Mrs. Stanche. I truly do."

CHAPTER 26
Wedding of the Season

Ruth Clarendon moved to Buffalo View Village to marry Mickey Blue Fox. Ruth's family would not attend her wedding. They, on the whole, did not approve of her choice for a husband. They'd never had a lawyer in the family and if they had to disown her to keep one out, they would. "All lawyers are shysters," they'd tell her. *Look in the mirror,* she'd think.

Ruth was a kind-hearted girl who loved her parents despite their attitudes and shady ways. However, she believed honesty and truthfulness to be of greater value than any financial gain achieved through trickery. She was upset by the treacherous thugs who attacked Mrs. Stanche, having seen firsthand, the damage done by those who will take what others have.

"She's so nice to me, Mickey. I can't stand to see her suffer."

Mickey drew Ruth close in his arms. "I wouldn't worry too much about Gloria Stanche. From what my dad says, she pulled it together pretty fast once she learned the truth about her mother and husband." He kissed Ruth on the top of her head. "Man, what a thing to wake up to on a morning!"

Ruth pulled away. "There's nothing funny about any of this. Don't joke!"

"Oh, I was not joking. Just imagining. One day your life is one way and when you wake up the next, it's totally different. And not in a good way!"

She snuggled into him again. "Like tomorrow." She smiled and kissed him.

"Yes, like tomorrow."

The young couple chose the evening of the Buffalo View Village Picnic to honor Mickey's forebearer's, Elmore and Sylvie, and their love for one another and their progeny. Ruth and Mickey hoped for six of their own progenies. Ruth, having been an only child, wanted a houseful of babies and Mickey, having grown up with five siblings of his own, wanted the same for his children. They had waited until marriage to consummate their love for one another but fully intended to start building that family before midnight on their wedding day.

At six fifteen p.m., on the day of her wedding, Ruth Clarendon arrived at the Episcopal church across the street from the picnic grounds. She was accompanied by two of her friends from the post office who agreed to be bridesmaids. Lucille Persons, looking luscious in a pastel blue, oversized floral print, cotton wrap dress, and a bold, white-beaded necklace, greeted them at the church door and escorted the women to the bride's changing room. She had a tray of lemonade, ice, champagne flutes, and vegetable hors d'oeuvres ready for them.

"Relax, ladies. I'll hang and steam your dresses. Ruth, take a deep breath, and if you need anything, I'll be right here. Oh, and Gloria called to say she will be here on time so not to worry about anything."

Gloria had arranged for an event planner to stage the picnic area and gazebo for the wedding. She received countless text updates, as she requested, to be prepared to abort any mishap that may be in process or impending. But everything was running smoothly. The caterers and the bar staff, the floral arrangements, and table settings, the chairs, the bridal approach, everything was in place by the time she arrived at seven p.m. She dashed into the church to see to Ruth, squeezing Lucille's hand in the doorway of the bridal room. Both women beamed happiness over Ruth and Mickey's joy.

"Is there anything else I can get for you, Ruth?" Gloria spoke softly so as not to startle the young woman who appeared to be deep in thought, holding a champagne flute forward from her face, yet not moving any muscle. Ruth moved her head slowly to the left so she could see Gloria.

"I believe I am so struck with happiness that I cannot move. So yes, break the spell, please!"

Everyone laughed and began to bustle about. "I'll help her with the finishing touches on her dress, Gloria. You can see to the preparations outside if you'd like."

Gloria left the dressing room to Lucille and the young ladies. She stood in the entryway of the church, looking across the street to the picnic grounds. Already there were guests filling chairs and tables, enjoying hors d'oeuvres, and drinks from the open bar. Mickey spared no expense to entertain his guests. For the most, these were people he'd known all his life. He was raised to respect his community and today he had an opportunity to show them a good time while he married his beloved Ruth.

"You know, son, you are the seventh generation of Blue Fox in this village." Roland was impeccably dressed in a tan, tailored suit with a purple shirt, a colorful beaded bolo at his neck, and he wore his spectacular maroon and silver boots. He stood behind Mickey, adjusting the boy's braid, and smoothing the shoulders of his tuxedo jacket.

"I'd forgotten, Pops. Are you about to hand me an ancestral bundle or something that binds me to a great spiritual task now that I am to be married?"

"You talk like you believe that a little." Roland grinned.

"I might. I know our people always talk about the seventh generation, but I guess I never thought of it as me."

"Well, you are the first generation now, building for the seven to follow. If we have done well by you, then you have much to be grateful for. It wasn't always good for us, you know."

"I do, Pops. And I am grateful." Mickey hugged his father. "We're going to make so many babies that the seventh generation will have to move the stars to make room for everybody."

Both men laughed, adjusted their ties, and stood tall, side-by-side. "Well, son, this is it. Let's go!"

The picnic grounds were now littered with camping chairs and coolers. Everyone in town was invited if they wanted to attend. The wooden folding chairs, cloth-draped tables, food and drink were reserved, however, for family and close friends. The wedding goers were noisier than they'd been as picnic goers, but better dressed. Mickey passed through the throng of guests, welcoming them, shaking hands, and thanking them for coming to show support for his marriage.

He took his position in the gazebo. To his right stood Reverend Persons. He nodded to Gloria Stanche as she took her seat next to the Reverend's wife. Both women smiled back at him then turned to visit with those seated nearest to them. Gloria reserved the chair to her right for Lester who was engaged in conversation with Roland near the front of the seating area. Roland patted Lester on the shoulder as the processional music began and trotted down the carpeted aisle to the back end of the runner. He had been honored by Ruth when she asked him to stand in for her father as the one to give her away. From the look on Roland's face as he wrapped Ruth's arm in his, there was no prouder moment in his life than this one.

There were sufficient speakers wired throughout the park so everyone could hear every word that was spoken. Even the children kept quiet while the short ceremony was in process. Women wept as the vows were shared between the young couple. And then it was over. Ruth and Mickey Blue Fox were announced as husband and wife. Their kiss brought a standing ovation and eruption of joyful noise from the crowd. Young lovers kissed in solidarity. This included an unexpected kiss from Ian McDougall onto the lips of June Franklin. And as expected, Lester Hill kissed Gloria Stanche, but with passion this time, leaving her lightheaded and open for more of the same.

Lucille felt a surge of jealousy. She was in love with Gloria and there was no way around it. Because of that love she was happy for Gloria. Finding Lester at just this time may have been the reason for her quick recovery from the recent traumatic events. Lucille had never been in love with a woman before. She hadn't known, or maybe not accepted, that a woman could feel sensual love for a man and a woman. She'd confessed her confusion to a favorite aunt in Philadelphia.

"Good for you, girlie!" Her aging aunt Pearl was a fan of the unconventional. She was also a lesbian. "So, this Gloria may not be for you, but you are still friends, right?"

"Yes. She is my best friend. I don't think I would have her in my life if it wasn't for my initial attraction."

"Good. Good. All of life comes with boundaries, right? There are beginnings and ends and middles in everything. You're in the middle with this Gloria, right?"

"I guess I am." Lucille began to relax.

"Okay then. And you still love your husband?"

"I do, Aunt Pearl, but the love has changed. When I met

Gloria, I felt a kind of excitement I've not experienced before. I can't just go back to being with my husband as we were."

"Do you need to leave him and start over?"

"I don't know. I promised myself I'd give it a little time. I do know the difference between infatuation and abiding love. I think infatuation distracted me from life-building with my husband. That's often where the divorce process begins, you know, with infatuation."

"There you go, girlie. Give it time. You know I'm always here for you, right?"

The consultation with her aunt helped Lucille frame a picture of her life with her husband and with Gloria in acceptable and achievable roles. The more she thought about the havoc a romantic infatuation can bring in a life, the more settled she felt about her decision to stay with her husband. Seeing the passionate kiss between Gloria and Lester, however, knocked a bit of wind out of her sails.

"This feeling will pass," she told herself. "Let it pass."

While the wedding of the year was in full celebration, a block away, in the city's court building, Morton, Lorinda, and Walter Stanche were being arraigned. Each pleaded not guilty to the long list of crimes leveled against them. Lester received a stream of texts from Claudia Yorke who had been assigned the courthouse beat for the evening. Sean McFee, receiving the text stream as well, converted the words to an official and publishable news report so he'd be ready the moment Lester gave him the go ahead.

"What are you doing on the phone so much?" Gloria, overcome by Lester's passionate kiss, was confused by his sudden inattentiveness.

"I'm sorry, Gloria, but I've got hot-off-the-press news breaking and I have to mentor my cub reporters through to the end of this one."

"It's the Stanches, isn't it?"

He took her face in his hands, kissing her again. "It is and you don't need to worry. You can read all about it tomorrow. Speaking of tomorrow, I'm wondering … Lester's voiced trailed off and his face flushed a little. "Gloria," Clearly nervous, he looked at her with a shy smile. "I've been wanting to ask you if you're ready, can I stay through breakfast?"

Gloria was stunned and relieved when Lester turned back to his texting. She had never been with any man other than Julian. She was older and though she was fit, her body, she knew was not youthful. *But he knows that*, she thought. And she wondered about the passionate kiss. She'd never felt anything like that before. How much different might love-making be with Lester?

He looked up from his phone and into Gloria's eyes. "You know this terrifies me." Gloria was torn between safety and bravery.

"I do."

"But I'm willing to try. We'll see how it goes." Gloria felt a lot of things in that moment. Hot, flustered, and afraid were at the top of the list.

"The arraignment is about done. I've given the kids the okay to write whatever they want. You and I should have some champagne and dance and congratulate the new couple. Let's see how that goes." His smile was impish and his kiss sweet.

At just that moment the Reverend Persons retrieved his wife. Lucille waved her goodbye to Lester and Gloria, knowing full well she must put an end to the romantic fascination with her friend and do all she could to recover love for her husband.

The next morning, Gloria woke next to Lester Hill, The Cat at her feet. A whispering breeze ruffled her bedroom curtains. She could not recall a time she had been this happy. She didn't want to move or cause anything to change. But The Cat was insistent.

"Okay. Okay." She snatched her robe from the reading chair and proceeded downstairs to feed her cat and start coffee.

Lester was not far behind and as the morning went on, over coffee, eggs, and biscuits, Gloria began to feel that they had been together forever. Every shred of hesitancy evaporated leaving ease and peace in its place.

CHAPTER 27
Julian Stanche is Put to Rest

"This is the day, huh?" Lester stirred a little sugar into his coffee. It was another warm, sunny summer day with a light breeze. "This weather is unbelievable. No wonder you people don't leave here."

"The winters are mild, too. We don't often have polar temperatures, although we've seen a few in the last few years. We do get a lot of snow."

"I love cross country skiing, and downhill, and winter sports in general, so that's fine with me."

"What about our getaway today? Should we decide on a destination or just go?"

"That's up to you, Gloria. I'm all for kicking about to see what happens. I do want to head southwest though. I've got some friends in a little town outside of Santa Fe that I want to see." He stood to refill his coffee cup.

"Wait, Lester. Let me fill a carafe and let's go outside."

Gloria's backyard was under construction. All the trenches had been filled and compressed. New patio blocks and irregular stone pathways were installed. Gloria opted against a fountain and chose instead a coy pond.

"I wish I'd done this before. Of course, had I done that, I

would have unearthed Julian. Then all manner of fortune hunters would have been crawling out of the woodwork." Gloria watched the coy slide beneath lily pads. "There was no good way for this to happen."

Gloria stared at the pond, watching a green frog leap in to take a swim. "The landscaper will bring in new plantings to surround the pond and he'll place a couple of wrought-iron benches over there and one here." Gloria pointed to concrete slabs on the freshly raked ground. "He should be done by the time we're back."

Lester took Gloria's hand. "You know, I was never one to pay attention to leaves and grass and all that. I was always too busy. But I like art. The way you talk about your gardens, it's like I'm on a museum tour. I like it." He kissed her on the cheek. "I also like coffee and I'd like mine before it's cold!"

Lester sat on a temporary chair at a temporary table and enjoyed his coffee while Gloria toured her gardens with The Cat at her heels. The cabbages were ready to harvest and the Swiss chard needed another cutting. Bright red beet tops and mature basil caused her heart to race. *There is so much to do.* She stopped herself from panic and returned to sit with Lester.

"My garden club has agreed to come by in shifts to care for the gardens and to harvest ripe vegetables and fruits for the community center dining hall. I'm not used to walking away from all this at the height of the season, but I want to. I want to do things differently — but not everything," she was quick to add with a bright smile. "I've told you that I like it here and I don't want my home to become a layover between trips to wherever."

"I understand that. I am willing to become settled here as well but I will not stop traveling. I don't have to be on the move all the time. Besides, those young reporters, as good as they are, will turn their jobs over to a new pair of students a year from now. I need to have the paper well established so I can hire a manager and be away as often as I like." Lester shifted forward in his chair. "But the digital age has made this entire thing so easy, who knows what I'll do with it in the future."

The couple sat in silence for a time. The Cat rested next to Gloria's feet with an eye on a bird taking a drink from the coy pond. "You will be a problem for this pond, my dear cat. That will take some figuring out." She whispered to her cat and bent over to scratch its ears. Instead of pouncing at the bird, The Cat closed its eyes in cat-like fashion and purred.

Meanwhile, miles away from Gloria's garden and thoughts, Detective Franklin and Sheriff McDougall gathered with Roland Blue Fox in his office.

"I never did understand what motivated Boone to capture the Stanches at the diner."

"Yeah," Blue Fox jumped in. "He called the local sheriff, Jasperson, to tell him that he suspected the two were up to no good after he saw the flashy old guy in the restaurant pass them an envelope. He didn't know they were Feds. He learned about the kidnapping from Jasperson. Good thing that happened, too. He had no cause to hog tie them. He got lucky on that one. And the fact that law enforcement across the state knows Boone. That more than anything kept him out of jail." Blue Fox, with one leg resting over the knee of the other, stroked a boot of dark brown leather with a striking black and silver pattern. "He is one lucky old man."

"It's over now. I worry, though, about Mrs. Stanche and her inheritance. Julian's interment is this afternoon. She will sign papers to receive seventy million dollars. She'll have a target on her every move." Franklin had been worrying about this from the moment Julian's body was found.

"I agree. There's going to be trouble." McDougall shook his head and frowned.

Roland assured them that they had nothing to worry about. "First, she's changing her name back to Shifton. No more Mrs. No more Stanche. And all the money will be in trust to various charities. She won't have access to any of it, other than a small amount of interest just to keep her flush throughout her life. We have a media plan, thanks to my good buddy, Lester Hill, to announce to the world how magnanimous and philanthropic she is, and we won't use her new name."

"That should work. I hope." Franklin had her doubts.

"Anything else before I break out the scotch?"

"Not a thing. I'd like to have a few under my belt before we go to court. Even if I have to testify, and I don't think that's going to happen, I could use fortification!" Franklin thanked Blue Fox for the first round and downed it in one swallow.

No one else but lawyers and a judge were required at the arraignment, no one but the defendants. Present as well was a member of the local press, young Claudia Yorke, who texted each step of the proceedings back to her cohort, Sean McFee.

Morton, Lorinda, and Walter Stanche were arraigned separately. The charges were numerous, from aiding and abetting to kidnapping to attempted murder and more. The judge denied bail, even though each one of them vigorously denied any involvement or complicity. Once arraigned, they were taken away until a court date could be arranged.

Next up was Detective Lorde, charged similarly and also denied bail. However, Lorde had been kept in solitary since his arrest. His status as a law enforcement officer put him at great risk from other inmates. His lawyer argued that Lorde had mental and other medical issues and therefore was entering a plea of not guilty. The judge listened, made notes, and denied bail, but agreed to keep him in solitary, "Although," the judge stated, "I don't see that's doing him much good." Lorde looked terrible. He was thin, unshaven, and wild-eyed as he stood before the judge.

"Can't tell if he's a good actor or crazy for real," texted Claudia.

Lester Hill stayed out of it as he'd assured Gloria he would. He was neither personally curious nor professionally interested. Lester liked to delegate and trusted the people he hired to do their jobs. He was, however, interested in helping Gloria make it through the day and out of town before sunset. He told her there was no plan, but he fibbed. A three-hour drive would take them to a cozy bed and breakfast for a relaxing beginning to their three-week trip.

Gloria fretted more about The Cat then she did an itinerary. "I know, Lucille, it's ridiculous. The Cat knows you almost as well as he knows me by now. I do feel strange about you staying in my house for that long a time without your husband."

"Oh, Gloria, my husband is a few blocks away. We're fine. The Cat will be fine. And just think, your freezer and larder will be full when you get back."

"I will call to check in and I'll send you photos."

"That would be great. I do want to ask one more time, though, do you want me at the interment?"

Gloria was quick to say no. "I want to get in and get out of that ritual and into the lawyer's office as fast as I can. I will be changing my name, by the way. I meant to tell you this before. I'm taking my mother's last name because it is, after all, my name. I want to be entirely rid of the Stanche association."

"That's a good idea, Gloria. Good for you."

"Gloria?" Lester entered the kitchen where Gloria was just getting off the call with Lucille. "Court is adjourned. They're all back in jail for now. No bail for any of them. Roland will meet us at the cemetery in an hour and then to his office and then we are out of here. Good?"

Gloria smiled at Lester. "So good. I need to finish packing and making notes for Lucille."

"I'm heading back to my place to get my things together. I'll be back here in 45 minutes."

"I can't wait. I feel like I'm holding my breath!"

There were few in attendance to send Julian on his way. Gloria wondered where he'd been all this time. Was he in purgatory like the Catholics believed? Was he roaming around town like a ghost waiting for his body to be blessed and buried? *What is death anyway?* Whatever this burial would mean, if anything, to Julian, it meant for Gloria that she could collect her marriage memories and her illusions about mother love and put them all to rest along with her husband. She knew at some point, she may feel regrets or sorrow, but that day was not this day. She was eager to say goodbye forever.

Reverend Persons clasped her hand as she stood next to him. "If you need anything after this, please call on us."

Gloria nodded and said she would do that. "I'm already taking your wife from you for three weeks."

Persons nodded. "And that is perfectly all right with us. We want to help you through this time in any way we can. The whole town feels that way."

Gloria removed her hand from Persons' grasp. "I know you are sincere, and I thank you so much."

"Let us begin."

As Father Persons spoke the words of Episcopal burial ritual, he and Gloria, Claudia Yorke, Lester Hill, and a gravedigger bowed their heads. At the last 'amen,' Gloria walked to the grave where Julian's casket was about to be lowered into a hole in the ground and covered up one more time, this time forever. She clutched a handful of soil then released it over the casket whispering words of forgiveness to Julian. "I know you didn't know what to do. I don't excuse your behavior, but I forgive you for it. I'm glad we're both free."

She thanked Father Persons and nodded to Yorke and the gravedigger, then turned her back on Julian's resting place and walked hand-in-hand with Lester Hill to his waiting car.

At Roland Blue Fox's office, Gloria signed the necessary papers for changing her name. They would be filed with the court on her return from traveling. She both received and dispersed the 70-million-dollar inheritance in a matter of minutes. She sat back with a sigh.

"There's one more thing." Roland handed her a letter.

Gloria looked concerned. "What is this about?"

"It's a letter from Julian."

"I don't want to read this. What does it say?"

Roland opened the letter and read it aloud.

Dearest Gloria. I never meant to hurt you. I know I was awful. I carry the pain I caused you in my heart. I'd like to believe that I would have told you eventually. But I am a coward and just couldn't do it. You will only read this if I have passed on. Hopefully, I will have had enough courage to be honest with you and you'll already know how sorry I am. Yours, Julian

Gloria began to laugh. Roland was stunned.

"Are you okay?"

Gloria tried to catch her breath, but the laughter overtook her. Roland poured her a glass of water. She managed to drink a little and calmed herself.

"I'm fine. I'm fine." She grinned. "It's just that, that letter is so Julian. There isn't a thing in it about me. It's all about him. Maybe there's reincarnation. Maybe he'll come back and try again. Maybe he'll be better. Maybe they all will." Gloria shook her head, stood and shook Roland's hand.

"Thank you for all you've done. I have a lovely man waiting for me outside and an opportunity for real love and some adventures, maybe. I'll see you in three weeks. Thank you again."

With that, Gloria left Roland's office to join her new love and begin her new life.

ABOUT THE AUTHOR

M E Fuller is a working writer and visual artist, currently residing in southwestern Minnesota. She is the recipient of grant support from Five Wings Arts Council and the Minnesota State Arts Board. Her first novel, *Saving the Ghost*, is a powerful story of survival and emotional healing.

For more information on M E Fuller, please visit her website at mefullerwords.com.

Made in the USA
Monee, IL
17 June 2021